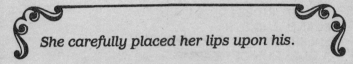

She carefully placed her lips upon his.

For one brief instant he jerked away. Then his mouth met hers roughly in an angry kiss that, the longer its duration, threatened to redirect its ferocity into something else. He seemed to sense the danger and at last managed to push her roughly away.

"Damn you, Mary Anne!"

"I am sorry, Anthony. I truly am. I didn't mean to bring on all of this."

"The hell you didn't."

Also by Marian Devon
*Published by Fawcett Books:*

MISS ARMSTEAD WEARS BLACK GLOVES
MISS ROMNEY FLIES TOO HIGH
M'LADY RIDES FOR A FALL
SCANDAL BROTH
SIR SHAM
A QUESTION OF CLASS
ESCAPADE
THE HEATHER AND THE BLADE
GEORGIANA

# FORTUNES
# OF
# THE HEART

## Marian Devon

FAWCETT CREST • NEW YORK

A Fawcett Crest Book
Published by Ballantine Books
Copyright © 1989 by Marian Pope Rettke

Library of Congress Catalog Card Number: 89-91122

ISBN 0-449-21596-2

Manufactured in the United States of America

First Edition: July 1989

# Chapter
# One

$M$iss Mary Anne Hawtry scrambled out of her stalled post chaise in the midst of the traffic that clogged Hyde Park Corner. "I'll walk the rest of the way," she shouted at the jarvey about the din arising from a baker's cart, a stagecoach, and a one-horse gig, whose drivers, each refusing to give way, were screaming insults at one another.

"You can bring my baggage over there." While pointing toward the second mansion from the corner, Miss Hawtry thrust some coins into the coachman's outstretched hand. Spurred on by the drizzle that threatened at any moment to change to full-blown rain, she gave a hike to the skirt of her gray traveling dress and began weaving her way through the throng of carriages, pedestrians, and horsemen at a pace scandalously close to a run. "Shoo!" She wheeled and stamped her foot at a small black-and-white mongrel who had joyfully given chase. As the dog obediently turned tail, she dashed up the marble steps that led to a pillared portico and banged away with the cast iron knocker.

The starchy butler's eyebrows elevated ever so slightly at the sight of the breathless, dampened young lady, but Miss Hawtry gave him no chance to speak. "My boxes are coming in that hackney, Carson." She gestured toward the black-and-yellow chaise that was at long last inching toward them. "Would you see to them, please?"

"Is Lady Cunliffe expecting you, miss?" the servant inquired with the barest touch of frost.

"No, it's a surprise. Where is my sister?"

"In her bedchamber. Preparing to go out, I believe."

But this time the butler's words were addressed to Miss Hawtry's back. She had pushed on past his august presence and was dashing up the stairs, where, after one peremptory rap at the bedchamber door, she unceremoniously flung it open.

The lady seated at the dressing table gave a startled gasp and dropped the rouge pot she was holding. "Oh, it's you. I'd thought—" She quickly recovered. "Mary Anne! What are you doing here? Don't you realize you could bring on heart failure, suddenly materializing this way?"

"Oh, I am sorry." Mary Anne looked anxiously at her beautiful sister, who seemed uncommonly pale. "You never used to be so nervy. Oh, my heavens! You thought I might be Maxwell, didn't you?" It did strike her that turning white as a ghost seemed an odd welcome for a husband who'd been away for ages fighting for his country. But then, since Sydney rarely allowed her emotions to show, her younger sister was in no position to judge them accurately.

"That will do for now, Clarissa." Lady Cunliffe smiled a dismissive smile at the dowdy middle-aged woman hovering over her. The dresser, whose artistry belied her looks, gave her mistress's coiffure, freshly curled and styled in the Gre-

2

cian manner, a last loving pat, made an unnecessary adjustment to the pink satin rosebuds that ornamented the left shoulder of her gauze-over-satin evening gown, cast a long, curious look at Miss Hawtry, then reluctantly left the room. Once the door had closed behind the servant, Lady Sydney Cunliffe turned on the dressing table bench to face her sister. "All right now, Mary Anne, out with it. Exactly why have you come here?"

"Is that any kind of greeting to give your only sister?" Mary Anne was removing her scarlet ostrich-plumed bonnet, revealing curls every bit as golden as Lady Cunliffe's, though not nearly so modishly dressed. She laid the headgear along with its matching reticule upon the canopied bed.

"I do hope those aren't wet. The counterpane's silk, you know."

"They aren't damp enough to hurt. Actually, I'm almost dry. And really, if I did not know better I should think you weren't glad to see me."

"You don't know better and I'm not." Sydney's exasperated smile took some of the sting from her words. "You were supposed to be in Bath for the entire summer. I repeat—what brings you here?"

"Isn't it obvious?" Mary Anne sat down upon a chaise lounge upholstered with the same pale blue of the bed and window hangings, the pervading color in the elegantly appointed white-and-gilded room. Though Sydney was only four years older than herself, the seniority had given her the knack of producing the dampening effect of an all-knowing governess upon demand. This apparently was to be one of those occasions. Mary Anne now steeled herself to meet her sister's cool appraisal.

"Oh, how could anyone be expected to stay in fusty old Bath with all this excitement going on in London?" the nine-teen-year-old protested. "Why the whole world's here for

3

the peace celebration . . ."—her gesture swept the globe—
"the Czar of all the Russias, the Grand Duchess of Oldenburg, the King of Prussia, General Blucher himself—to name
merely a few. And then when the papers reported that my
famous brother-in-law, General Cunliffe—who had as much
to do with oversetting Napoléon as anyone, I daresay—was
to be in town as well. . . . Oh, really, Sydney, you couldn't
be so cruel as to expect me to miss all this excitement, now,
could you?"

"Ah, the truth is about to out." Sydney turned back to
give her toilette a final appraisal in the looking glass. There
was little to find fault with. The enormous gray eyes, rose-
petal complexion, and classic features were quite as perfect
as her latest coiffure. She frowned a bit at her pallor, though,
and picked up the rouge pot she'd dropped earlier.

"Why are you using that stuff? You never used to."

"As an antidote to being startled out of my wits." She
applied a tiny bit, blended it carefully, then left the dressing
table to sit beside her sister. "And did the paper also just
happen to mention that your famous brother-in-law would be
accompanied from France by his military aide, a certain
Captain Anthony Rodes?"

"Well, yes," Mary Anne admitted. "Among others. And
I knew that if you were having a house party, Sydney darling,
you'd want me here. I just anticipated your letter of invitation, that's all."

Sydney gave her sister another governess look, then sighed.
"There was not going to be a letter of invitation, Mary Anne,
as I suspect you realize. For, I assure you, what with mixing
Max's guests with the two Prussian dignitaries the govern-
ment has asked me to house—who by the by haven't a word
of English between them—things will be quite awkward
enough without having the woman who turned down Captain
Rodes's proposal of marriage here as well. And I suppose

your tiresome fiancé has come with you. Oh, God, does he expect to stay here, too? You did write me that he's leased out his town house? Well, I collect we'll manage somehow. But he may have to sleep with the Prussians.''

Mary Anne was looking at her sister rather oddly. ''What do you mean 'tiresome fiancé'? I thought you approved of Roderick.''

''Of course I do. Who wouldn't approve of twelve thousand pounds per year, with a title thrown in for good measure?''

''You sound just like Mama.''

''No need to act so surprised. Aren't the three of us made from one mold?''

''Well, yes, I suppose so'' came the reluctant admission. ''At least Anthony always said that *you* were just like Mama.''

''Did he indeed?'' The delicately arched eyebrows rose. ''But then the vicar's son never did approve of me, did he? Well, now he's even less reason to approve of you. Which makes your arrival here rather worse than awkward. Oh, well, under the circumstances, what's one more coil. I'll simply ring for Carson and let him solve the problem of where to put Lord Littlecote. By the by, what have you done with him in the meantime?''

''He's still in Bath.''

''Well, heaven be praised for that. But I must confess I'm amazed. I'd hardly have expected your possessive fiancé to allow you to cut your visit short and come haring up to London. Will wonders never cease.''

''He didn't *allow* me to come.'' Mary Anne took a deep breath, squared her shoulders, and forced herself to meet her sister's eyes. ''Actually, Roderick had nothing to say in the matter. He's no longer my fiancé. I've cried off, you see.''

''Good God!'' Sydney stared at her sister in horror. ''Have

5

you taken leave of your senses, Mary Anne? He was the catch of a lifetime!''

"I know." She looked miserable. "Please don't you ring a peal over me. Leave that for Mama. And don't try to reason with me either." She held up a hand to forestall any lecture. "I know I'm completely sap-skulled, but I can't help myself. I just can't love him, don't you see."

"I'm afraid I do see, actually." Lady Cunliffe was regarding her sister with a knowing expression. "You've somehow learned of Anthony's fortune. I was hoping that you would not."

"Anthony's what?"

"Please, Mary Anne. For heaven's sake, spare me your guileless looks. I feel the headache coming on. Somehow or other you've got wind of Anthony's inheritance and you're here to try and get him back. Oh, really, little sister, I wish you'd turn right around and head for Bath. It's much too— ouch!"

Her words were cut short as her sister clutched her arm. "Sydney, will you please stop rattling and explain yourself. What fortune? What inheritance?"

"Control yourself. If I'm not bruised, it will be a miracle." She rubbed her forearm gingerly.

"Sydney!"

"Oh, please do not play games with me. Save that sort of thing for your captain if you must. Naturally I'm speaking of the fortune Anthony inherited from his uncle. As if you didn't know."

"Well, I didn't know!" came the indignant response. "I didn't even know he *had* an uncle. A rich one at any rate. Oh, my goodness! Now I remember! The black sheep in Brazil! He made a fortune? And left it to Anthony? Oh, I say! How famous!" she crowed with delight, then suddenly looked stricken. "Oh, my goodness. It isn't famous at all, though, is it? In fact, it's terrible. He'll think I knew it all along."

"And didn't you?" Her sister's voice was cynical.

"No, I didn't," the other wailed. "I'd not the slightest inkling of anything of the kind. All I knew was that the moment I got over the triumph of actually landing a catch like Lord Littlecote and then contemplated having to live the rest of my life with someone I didn't love while constantly thinking of somebody I did, well, it just didn't seem fair to anybody. So then I read that Anthony was coming back to England, I knew what I had to do. I just left a note for Littlecote and ran. But believe me, I had no notion that Anthony would ever inherit anything."

Sydney studied her sister's stricken face and sighed. "Yes, actually, I think I do believe you."

"Well, Anthony won't. I know it. For when I turned down his marriage offer, you see, I told him it was because I'd every intention of marrying a fortune."

"That should hardly have come as a surprise," Sydney remarked dryly. "Our mother's views on the subject were well-known."

"Actually, it was a surprise. For he knew I loved him. And he felt that should outweigh the other and that we should be able to manage on his lieutenant's pay. He said some terrible things to me. He told me I was a cold-blooded little schemer just like you."

"Knowing Captain Rodes's true opinion of me is bound to make his visit here so much more enjoyable," Sydney murmured.

"Well, I'm sorry. I should not have repeated that. Besides, you mustn't blame him too much, for it was all my fault. I'd told him, don't you see, that I was determined to make as good a match as you'd done." She paused a moment to reflect. "And to think I almost pulled it off."

"Oh, come now. You surely aren't comparing that widgeon Littlecote with Lieutenant General Sir Maxwell Cunliffe? Don't be absurd."

"I most certainly am. Oh, I know Roderick's no military hero, but a viscount does outrank a baronet, you must admit."

"I doubt his fortune is as large, though, since Maxwell is a nabob, but it's certainly not paltry. By the by, do you know the size of Anthony's inheritance?"

"Oh, every bit as large as Littlecote's, or so I've heard."

"That much!" Mary Anne's face fell. "I was hoping it was less. Then Anthony would know I was marrying him for his own sake and not for his money. Oh, well," she brightened, "I'll just have to convince him of it, won't I?"

"Go back to Bath, Mary Anne." There was real concern in Sydney's voice. "Apologize to Littlecote. Tell him you simply wished to make him jealous or something of the sort. I know you don't love him now, but perhaps in time you can learn to do so. I'm sorry if I called him tiresome. And a widgeon. I should not have done. I suspect he's actually quite a good sort. I've never heard otherwise. And you're right, you know. He is a marvelous catch."

"Sydney, you're actually babbling. Out with it. What's the matter? You don't think I can bring Anthony around, do you? Well, I'll just have to, that's all. Besides, you're forgetting one thing. I may have made him furious, but I know he loves me. He's done so since we were in leading strings."

"But two years is a long time, Mary Anne. Anything can happen."

"Well, it wasn't long enough for me to stop loving him, and God knows I really worked at it."

"Go back to Bath. Right now. Before they all get here."

"Sydney, whatever's wrong? What aren't you telling me?"

"I don't know how to break this gently, Mary Anne." The sister's voice was filled with pity. "Anthony's betrothed.

To an heiress. The daughter of a diplomat. He met her in Portugal. She's traveling in Maxwell's party. And will be staying here. So you see, my dear, how impossible this situation—Mary Anne!'' Her voice rose in alarm. ''Surely you aren't about to faint?''

''Don't be absurd,'' the other answered thickly. ''I've never had the vapors in my life. However, I do believe I'm about to cast up my accounts.''

Sydney took one look at the pale countenance that was rapidly taking on a greenish cast and made a mad dash across the chamber to the washstand. She snatched up a flowered porcelain basin and returned with it to her sister's side in the barest nick of time.

# Chapter
# Two

"*How are you feeling?*" Lady Cunliffe anxiously surveyed her sister, who was propped up in bed sipping her morning tea.

"Oh, top of the trees." Mary Anne managed to smile though the dark circles under her eyes and her sickly pallor belied both the expression and the words. "But what on earth are you doing up and dressed so early?" The hands of the ormolu clock on the mantelpiece had not quite reached the hour of nine. "You were out terribly late last night, weren't you?"

"Keeping tabs on me?"

"Nothing of the kind. I just wondered that you didn't get your beauty sleep."

"I collect that's a tactful way of saying I look hagridden." Sydney sat down upon the foot of the four-poster bed. "But it's quite unnecessary. I'm well aware of it."

"Don't be absurd. You couldn't possibly look hagridden."

And it was true, Mary Anne thought with a mental sigh. Sydney's rather drawn look and the sooty smudges beneath her eyes only added to her etherealness, making her look like one of the more interesting heroines of a gothic novel. Whereas for herself—the dull throbbing in her temples coupled with the fact she'd tossed and turned the whole night long were enough to warn her to shun any more contact with the looking glass than was absolutely necessary.

Sydney seemed to read her mind. "Oh, don't worry, little sister. You'll do. But I'm hoping that after a night's reflection you've changed your plans. I'm here to offer you my coach to take you back to Bath."

"No, thank you." Under the exasperated scrutiny of her sister, Mary Anne took another sip of scalding tea. She picked up a light-wig and buttered it, but then had second thoughts. Trying to repress a shudder, she put the roll back upon her plate.

"Not feeling quite the thing, I see. Well, forgive my plain speaking, but matters can only get worse if you insist upon staying. Be reasonable, Mary Anne. Anthony's betrothed. The notice was in the papers."

"*I* didn't see it."

"Well, even if it wasn't publicized in the provinces, it's written in stone nonetheless."

"A betrothal isn't a marriage. As I should know."

"In this case it's as good as," Sydney said flatly. "I don't know what sort of fantasy you're weaving, but even if Anthony Rodes does show up here to fall head over heels in love with you again—oh, all right, then, *still*, if you insist," she amended in response to a gurgle of protest into the teacup, "you have to remember, he's a gentleman. And no gentleman cries off."

"I realize that. Then *she'll* have to do so, that's all."

"Why ever should she? If you suddenly eliminated all the marriages of our class where the bride and groom didn't love each other, the population would drop alarmingly." And with that cynical observation Sydney climbed down from the high bed.

"Well, I've done my sisterly duty and won't waste any more time in warnings you aren't going to pay the slightest attention to. The role of Cassandra doesn't really suit me. Besides which, I've far too much to do. Between the master's arrival and the dinner party I'm giving tonight, the servants are on their ears."

"You're giving a party tonight?" Mary Anne was astounded. "Whatever for?"

"Why, to welcome the conquering hero of course."

"But I should think that on his first night home he'd prefer the two of you to be alone," her sister blurted.

"Oh, I think not. If that were true, he'd be coming alone, now, wouldn't he? No, I'm sure he'd find it odd if there were no reception. So I've prosed on long enough here. And if you're quite determined to stay, Mary Anne, believe it or not, well, I am glad to have you." She impulsively bent over and kissed her sister on the forehead.

"Really truly?" Mary Anne raised a skeptical eyebrow.

"Certainly. Misery loves company, as they say. Now then, there's no need for you to be involved in the general uproar. Why not try and get some sleep? It's going to be a very, very long day, little sister."

But after the door had closed behind Sydney, Mary Anne failed to take her advice. Instead she poured herself another cup of tea and sipped it thoughtfully. And for the first time since her arrival at Cunliffe House her mind broke free from the muddle of her own affairs to dwell on her sister's odd behavior.

When the beautiful and dowerless Miss Sydney Hawtry had come up from the country and had snared that most elusive, highly eligible bachelor, Sir Maxwell Cunliffe, it had been considered a triumph rated somewhere between Cinderella's capture of the handsome prince and the London conquests of the fabled Irish Gunning sisters.

The courtship had been of the whirlwind variety. The couple was joined in wedlock and after the briefest of honeymoons the groom had gone back to the peninsula to rejoin his regiment. He had managed to get a short leave for the birth of his child, and that had been the extent of Sir Maxwell and Lady Cunliffe's life together. There had been plans for Sydney and Savannah to join him abroad. But then the rigors of the campaign against the Corsican Monster had made that impossible.

Mary Anne had met her brother-in-law at the wedding and had been overawed. In the first place, the groom was fifteen years older than her sister and therefore seemed an ancient. In the second, Sir Maxwell's reputation as a soldier was beginning to soar. He was thoroughly lionized in his London stay. She had given very little thought to how Sydney might feel about her husband. She only knew how ecstatic their mother had been over the match. It had become a standard for the younger daughter to strive for.

Certainly her sister's life had seemed all that anyone could ever wish for. Sydney had become the instant toast of London. She was constantly surrounded by a bevy of Bond Street beaux delighted to dangle after a beautiful married lady who posed no threat to their liberty. There was keen competition among them for the honor of escorting Lady Cunliffe to the opera, the theater, Almack's, and to all the private entertainments the London Season offered.

If she had considered the matter at all, Mary Anne would have been convinced that her sister was very happy. Now she began to wonder. What had Sydney said about loveless marriages? Could it be that she'd actually lost her heart to one of the gentlemen who squired her around the town? The thought was unsettling. For somehow Sydney, a cool, aloof ice maiden, seemed above that sort of thing.

" 'Ave you finished, miss?''

Mary Anne's musings were mercifully cut short by the young maid who'd come to fetch her tray. And knowing that further sleep would prove impossible, she rose and dressed with unaccustomed care.

The results were mixed. She was inordinantly pleased with the way Clarissa, who had volunteered her services, had arranged her hair. The dresser had firmly overridden Mary Anne's suggestion that she copy Sydney's style. No, Miss Hawtry must have her own coiffure. The effect was very French. A profusion of blond ringlets was brought low on the sides of her face while the back hair was swept up to form a crown of curls. Clarissa then added a spray of cornflowers that matched both the blue of Mary Anne's eyes and the sprigged muslin of her favorite morning gown, which in spite of all the household flurry had been unpacked and smoothed for her.

But her pleasure in her coiffure was short-lived. As her eyes traveled downward in the cheval glass, she had to admit that Sydney's term "hagridden" best described her own face. And unlike her sister, she concluded, she looked merely tired, not romantically drawn and wasted. She pulled a face at her reflection and went in search of Sydney.

She found her in the kitchen, in conference with the cook. "Why don't you entertain Savannah for a bit and free up Betsy to help the maids," she responded absently to Mary Anne's offer of assistance. This was the perfect task. It was impossible to remain blue-deviled around a two-year-old.

As Mary Anne headed toward the nursery she passed two

strange gentlemen upon the stairs. One, middle-aged and distinguished, was wearing a foreign uniform; the other, fair-haired and pleasant-looking, was dressed in civilian clothes. Their heavily accented "good mornings" confirmed that these were the Prussian houseguests Sydney had mentioned.

Mary Anne was greeted with squeals of delight by her tiny niece and with relief by the nursemaid who'd been trying to help out in the household crisis with a toddler underfoot. "Why don't I take her out a bit?" she suggested.

"Oh, best to ask her ladyship first, miss. She told me most particular not to let Miss Savannah muss herself, seeing as how her father hasn't clapped eyes on his only child since she was a tiny squalling infant."

When Mary Anne finally located her sister in the with-drawing room arranging flowers, Sydney did agree to the outing, but with the same caveat: "Do keep her tidy, Mary Anne. I'm sure it's a big enough disappointment to Maxwell that Savannah's not a son. Let's not have her looking like a hoyden."

"Don't talk like that in front of her." Mary Anne frowned. "You sound for all the world like Mama."

"Well, why not?" Sydney replied absently as she backed off to study the arrangement of yellow roses in their silver basket. "She was right in that much at least. It is a man's world, no mistake. Certainly our lives would have been much smoother if one of us had been a male. We would not have lost the estate when Papa died."

"Well, Sir Maxwell is a fool if he wants this one to be otherwise." Mary Anne spoke with conviction as she scooped her small niece out from underneath the Pembroke table where she'd just crawled.

"She is rather special, isn't she?" Sydney smiled fondly at the golden-haired, pink-cheeked child. "Run along with your auntie, precious. And mind you, stay clean. Your papa's coming home."

"Papa come home," Savannah echoed as she dutifully put her hand in Mary Anne's. They left the house and headed toward the park.

It did not take long to doubt the wisdom of the outing. It had seemed reasonable enough to agree to go on an expedition to see the ducks as she was tying on the child's poke bonnet and the sun was sparkling on the windowpanes. But once outdoors it became evident that the previous day's rain had left an aftermath of mud and puddles. Mary Anne looked dubiously at her small charge's white stockings and soft pink shoes, the exact shade of the muslin gown she wore, and briefly considered going back for pattens. Oh, well, if they were careful. She picked the child up in her arms and dashed across Hyde Park Corner, taking advantage of a sudden lull in traffic.

Mary Anne was appalled at the transformation in the park. A carnival atmosphere obscured the natural beauty of the scene. Tents and booths had sprouted everywhere like giant toadstools. Preparations for the mock naval engagement that would soon take place upon it had robbed the serpentine of its serenity. Ugly scaffolding for fireworks defaced its banks.

But none of this diverted the child from her single-minded purpose. "Go feed ducks," Miss Cunliffe declared.

"We can't," her aunt replied reasonably. "We didn't bring anything to feed them. Besides, it's too muddy down by the water, and you'd ruin your pretty shoes."

"Want to feed ducks!"

Mary Anne looked hastily around to find a likely distraction. She had just settled upon a booth featuring both toy drums and bugles and was wondering, first, if she had enough money in her reticule to cover the inevitably inflated prices of the toys, and, second, if Sydney would murder her if she bought one of the rackety things, when Savannah wriggled out of her grasp and went racing toward the feathered flock circling the water.

"Savannah, come back here!"

The child's full attention was upon the ducks, who, expecting a meal, were scrambling up onto the bank, quacking noisily. She failed to heed her aunt's command or notice the bare patch in the grass that last night's rain had turned into a mud slide. Just as Mary Anne lunged for her and missed, the child's feet flew out from underneath her and she sprawled full-length upon her back. Squalling as much in indignation as from pain, Savannah rolled over and pushed herself upright with her palms.

Mary Anne gazed with horror at her mud-coated niece. Savannah, looking down at her ruined frock and shoes, grasped the full enormity of what had happened and cried harder. Her aunt stifled the "Now look what you've done" that hovered on her tongue. The notion of dipping the toddler in the serpentine also died aborning. Instead, she followed her instincts and put her arms around the sobbing child. "There, there. Accidents happen. It's not the end of the world, you know. We'll just have to get you home and cleaned up before your papa arrives, now, won't we?" And before your mama sees you, she added in a silent prayer. With an inward sigh for her own favorite sprigged muslin, donned particularly to dazzle Captain Rodes, she picked up the child and in a half run half walk headed toward Cunliffe House.

The Corner was even more traffic-jammed than usual. She waited impatiently for an opening, then scooted across the street while Savannah continued to intone "Pity shoes all muddy" over and over and over, a doleful litany.

" 'Pity' Savannah and Mary Anne all muddy. I'd settle gladly for the shoes."

Just as she'd leapt the curbstone Mary Anne spied an open

barouche slowing to a stop in front of her sister's residence. "Oh, no! Please don't let it be!" she breathed. The coach contained four passengers, two females who rode facing two military gentlemen. And though Mary Anne was not familiar with the uniform of the Life Guards, she was reasonably sure that no one more lowly than a general would sport such plumes and gold upon his bicorne as one officer was wearing.

She was just about to turn tail, dash around behind Apsley House, and then approach their own dwelling from the servants' entrance, when the tall man climbing out of the carriage turned and saw them. The haughty face, dominated by a hawkish nose and eyes that could pierce like a blue-steel sword blade, suddenly softened. "Sydney!" he called out but then quickly qualified. "Why, no, I'm mistaken. It must be Mary Anne, all grown up now. But can this possibly be my baby girl?"

With some difficulty Mary Anne pulled her attention away from another pair of blue eyes and a face rigid with shock back to her brother-in-law. "Yes, it's Savannah, sir. But I'm afraid we've had a mishap involving a mud puddle and some ducks. I was hoping to clean her up before you arrived. We'll only be a moment."

"Nonsense. She's perfect the way she is."

Savannah had twisted in her aunt's arms and was gazing solemnly at the tall stranger. She removed a thumb, now the only clean spot upon her, in order to inform him, "Pity shoes all muddy."

"So I see," the gentleman replied with equal solemnity. "Could you come and give your papa a kiss?" And he knelt down and held out his arms.

There was no help for it. Mary Anne set her small charge down upon the cobblestones. Without a second's hesitation Savannah made a beeline for the outstretched arms. "Oh, do be careful," Mary Anne gasped, but the warning went unheeded. The general was soon involved, with every evidence of enjoyment, in an enthusiastic bear hug. And when he stood up again with the toddler in his arms he seemed not in the least perturbed by his mud-streaked uniform or the fact that his cheek was smeared from a muddy kiss.

If he really wanted a son like Sydney says, he hides it well, Mary Anne thought inanely while she studiously avoided looking at the other officer who had just helped a young lady from the coach while her maid climbed down unassisted.

"If you'll excuse me," she murmured, "I must see about—"

"Oh, but first you must meet my guests." The general was used to being obeyed and preempted Mary Anne's impulse to bolt. "I can assure you they have both seen mud before.

"Lady Barbara, may I present my sister-in-law, Miss Hawtry. Lady Barbara Kennet. And this gentleman is my aide, Captain Anthony Rodes. Anthony, Miss Hawtry. Oh, but of course. I had forgot. You two already know each other. Grew up as neighbors I believe Sydney wrote me."

"That's right, sir," Captain Rodes replied woodenly. His eyes coolly appraised the muddy mess that had caused him countless hours of heartbreak while his face revealed no clue to whatever he might be feeling. "How do you do, Miss Hawtry."

As for Mary Anne, when she looked into the shuttered eyes of this military stranger, she was beset by a whole battalion of emotions. She wanted to shake him back to life, she wanted to scream, she wanted to cry, she wanted to sink. Then, finally, more than anything, she wanted to match his cool aloofness. But instead of replying to his greeting with the same detached formality, "Why ever did you grow a mustache?" she blurted out.

# Chapter
# Three

M iss Mary Anne Hawtry spent the remainder of the day skulking in her chamber, lying on the bed, trying to keep at bay a welter of impressions. But her racing brain was no respecter of her churning emotions and kept popping up images anyway and forcing her to confront them.

There were the dagger looks, for instance, that Sydney had thrown her way as she came to greet the arrivals in the hallway and had seen Savannah's state. Mary Anne now contrasted that impassioned glare with the reserved correctness of the welcome she had given her long-absent husband. And the chaste kiss the general had planted upon her sister's cheek (here Mary Anne winced as she recalled the smudge of mud he'd transferred to Sydney's cool perfection) was as great a contrast to the enthusiastic bearhug with which he'd greeted his little daughter.

And Lady Barbara Kennet's image kept perversely reappearing, although Mary Anne would have much preferred to think about her ladyship at some later time. For now she recognized the fact that, without realizing it, she had conjured up several tolerable descriptions of Anthony's fiancée in the brief time she'd known of her existence. Lady Barbara fit none of them.

It had not been realistic, of course, to hope she'd be as plain as sin with a huge wart on her nose and a decided squint. But then reality had not brought the kind of beauty either that had been her second choice. She had longed for a type who was spoiled and haughty, looking down her titled nose at all inferiors. For Anthony—unless he'd changed past recognition, a possibility she was now prepared to entertain—would despise that.

The real Lady Barbara had turned out to be trim and neat, with intelligent gray eyes and a nice complexion. Her only claim to beauty lay in her thick, shiny chestnut-colored hair. It was enough. And far from appearing conceited and proud, she'd proved the soul of amiability. She had thought Savannah the most delightful of children. She had smiled sympathetically at Mary Anne's sprigged-muslin ruin during an awkward explanation of the consequences of ducks and mud. Mary Anne groaned aloud at the memory. For Lady Barbara Kennet had seemed—nice. This was the most devastating adjective she could ever apply to anyone betrothed to Captain Rodes.

And as for that traitorous gentleman—here, with a supreme effort of will, Mary Anne did manage one degree of mind over matter. She absolutely would not allow herself to think of Anthony just yet. She would dress for dinner instead.

This time Mary Anne did not fuss over her appearance. After the initial impression she'd made, it hardly seemed to matter. Her much-worn white gros de Naples gown looked well enough. She added the single strand of pearls Sydney had given her on her come-out, touched up her hair herself, added a garland of damask roses, thanked the nervous maid, and squared her shoulders to face whatever came.

As she entered the gold-striped drawing room she was glad to see that most of the guests were already assembled there. Some magnate pulled her gaze immediately to Anthony, who, with Lady Barbara by his side, was listening attentively to a stout dowager top-heavy with purple plumes. Something caused him to raise his head and look her way. But when their eyes met, he quickly averted his while Mary Anne's spirits sank even lower. She took a deep breath then, fixed a bright smile in place, and deliberately chose to join the group of people positioned farthest away from the man she was in love with.

Immediately she wished she'd been more discriminating. "Ah, the other beautiful Miss Hawtry," a voice said.

The exquisite with the obscuring circle of attentive listeners around him broke off recounting the Regent's latest national embarrassment to greet the newcomer while he appraised her with a not-quite-veiled amusement. "Up from the country I see, to hail the conquering hero. Or conquering *heroes*, perhaps I should say?" He gestured with his quizzing glass vaguely in the direction of Captain Rodes.

Mary Anne could never dredge up sufficient cause for disliking Lord Linley Mortlock so intensely. He was a tulip of fashion, a pink of the *ton*, an amusing raconteur, an excellent dancer, a nonesuch at cards, and therefore much in demand by fashionable hostesses. Moreover, he was a bosom beau and confidant of Lady Sydney Cunliffe and her most frequent escort about the town. It was this last fact, Mary Anne now admitted to herself, that could have been the chief cause of her irrational dislike.

Of course there was nothing at all improper in the attachment. Lord Linley was Sir Maxwell Cunliffe's cousin, hence a logical choice of squire to the absent soldier's wife. The kinship should have sufficed to silence the gossip-mongers. But Mary Anne was well aware that it had not.

Just as dinner was announced by a powdered footman, Lord Linley concluded his malicious anecdote that had cast equal discredit upon the Crown Prince and his appalling wife. He then turned to Mary Anne. "Your sister has commanded me to take you in to dinner. And I was wondering how to find you in the crush." His languid wave encompassed the packed room. "Where does Sydney find these creatures? Well, never mind. It is extremely considerate of you to spare me the tedium of searching for you. Most females are not so obliging. They seem to think it one's moral duty to track them down and therefore try and make it as difficult as possible, believing it adds to their consequence if a partner has to look underneath the furniture and behind the draperies. So I thank you for doing the searching out yourself, Miss Hawtry."

"Oh, but I didn't—" She broke off in confusion before his mocking smile. "You were merely funning, weren't you?"

"Only attempting to, it seems."

He offered an arm and Mary Anne placed a white kid glove gingerly upon it. She suddenly realized he knew she disliked him. And that bit of insight furnished at least one reason for it. Lord Linley Mortlock was, by far, too knowing. He seemed to see right through one.

She was convinced it was an act of pure mischief on her escort's part to choose a place far down the enormous polished table exactly opposite Captain Rodes and Lady Barbara. For she had no doubt at all that he was aware of her past history. Sydney must have told him of it the evening before when he'd escorted her to the ball given for the Russian Czar and the Grand Duchess. Mary Anne longed to put a flea in her sister's ear. Suddenly she felt a lot less guilty for allowing that paragon's baby daughter to turn into a mud lark.

Across the table, as though she'd picked up Mary Anne's train of thought, Lady Barbara was telling the story of her introduction to her host and hostess's enchanting, muddy little girl. Though the anecdote was for the benefit of a grandmotherly type who'd asked how old the general's child was, for want of conversational topics of their own all within earshot listened.

"You must have been something of a mess yourself." Lord Linley addressed Mary Anne in a carrying aside. "How it must have distressed you to be out of countenance. For I'm sure you were eager to make a good impression. It's been how long now since you've seen your soldier hero?" He looked deliberately toward Captain Rodes and smiled his slow, enigmatic smile.

"I had not seen *Sir Maxwell* since my sister's wedding." Mary Anne forced herself to meet his mocking gaze though all the while she was conscious of Anthony's attention. Well, at any rate he'd see that she was paired with one of the most handsome men in London. Lord Linley, with his fair hair, pale eyes, and Greek god features, was more often misidentified as Sydney's cousin rather than her husband's. But just what Anthony would think of his exquisite good looks and effete manner did not really bear considering.

Were it not for the combined efforts of Lady Barbara and Lord Linley, socialization at their portion of the table would have been at a standstill. For the most part, Captain Rodes kept his attention fixed upon his plate. But during the progression of removes he spent more time rearranging its contents than eating. At first, Mary Anne was herself struck dumb by the reality of his presence after he'd haunted her thoughts for two long years. Then gradually she grew angry at being ignored. "I collect you must find our English weather very different from Spain's, Captain Rodes" was the brilliant conversational opening directed across the table.

His face was blank enough to have been carved in granite. But the blue eyes impaled her for a long deliberate moment before he answered. "*Very* different? Why, no, Miss Hawtry." His voice was a flagrant imitation of Lord Linley's affected drawl. "Both have many of the same elements—sunshine, clouds, rain, wind, and the like. Nothing we haven't as yet heard of."

Lord Linley chuckled as at some sparkling witticism, though Mary Anne was sure he realized that he, too, was being mocked. Lady Barbara gave her fiancé a startled look. But the captain had deliberately turned his attention to the lady on his left and was now engaging her in conversation.

Mary Anne felt her cheeks grow hot at the blatant set-down. At the earliest opportunity she managed to stretch a leg far enough beneath the table to plant a kick on her true love's silk-stockinged shin. There was some gratification in seeing him jump. But less in being the recipient of a look filled with venom. Well, if she had not precisely known how things stood between them up to that point, there was no doubt left about it now.

Lord Linley had not missed the exchange. "Tell me, Miss Hawtry," he asked in a voice calculated to preempt all other conversations among their table mates, "where is Lord Littlecote keeping himself? It's most unusual for him not to be dancing attendance upon you."

"He's in Bath." Her tone was meant to put a period to that particular topic. Even though his attention was apparently upon his dinner companion, she could see Anthony's ears prick up.

His lordship, though, was not inclined to drop the subject. "Can the rumors possibly be true, then, that you have broken your engagement? The gossip-mongers are all saying you're in love with someone else."

"And you listened to them? You amaze me, sir. You of all people should know better than to place any value upon such tittle-tattle. I for one am convinced that the chief practitioners of gossip make up their stories as they go along in order to create as much mischief as they can."

"Touché," he murmured, smiling across his wineglass. "Still, I am amazed that Lord Littlecote would allow his bride-to-be so much freedom. With all these army officers in town he must be secure indeed to risk having his fiancée tumble head over heels in love with a splendid uniform."

Mary Anne toyed with the idea of planting the second swift kick of the evening but soon thought better of it. Lord Linley would be certain to remark on the event to everyone around them.

But at least for the moment that gentleman seemed satisfied with the havoc he'd created in her composure and turned his attention to the lady on his left. And Mary Anne followed the example set by her childhood's boon companion and concentrated upon the food upon her plate. The French beans looked best where the broiled mushrooms had been. Carving the meat away from a chicken wing in tiny bites was also time-consuming.

Across the table Lady Barbara, placed next to one of the Prussian gentlemen, was conversing with him in his own tongue, much to that gentleman's delight. And since everyone else around was also engaged in talk with the exception of herself and Anthony, Mary Anne stared hard at him until he finally raised his eyes from the dissection of his pheasant. She gave him a smile intended to convey an apology for the damage she'd done his shin. There was no answering change in his expression. His attention refocused on his plate. She suppressed a sigh and shifted her French beans and the broiled mushrooms back to their original positions.

The meal dragged on forever through its three removes. Sir Maxwell, playing host, looked weary and somewhat less than enthralled by the conversation around him. Indeed his attention often seemed to wander to the opposite end of the long table where his wife sparkled with wit and from the diamonds and the silver-threaded gauze she wore.

Indeed her ladyship appeared to be doing her animated best to compensate for her spouse's somber mood. And well she should, Mary Anne thought censoriously. I knew that giving this party so soon was a shatter-brained idea. No one was more relieved than she when her brother-in-law at last caught her sister's eye and Sydney stood to signal that it was time for the ladies to withdraw. And Mary Anne did not care in the least if her own hasty departure resembled a retreat. For the first time she felt a sympathy for Napoléon.

The ladies were not left to their own devices for long, however. Instead of lingering over their port, the gentlemen joined the fair sex in the withdrawing room with remarkable alacrity. Their promptness possibly indicated some desire on Sir Maxwell's part to get the evening over with.

Dancing and cards were planned. After Sir Maxwell had chosen the latter, as perhaps the lesser evil, his cousin, with an elaborate bow, led Lady Cunliffe out upon the floor to signal a cotillion. And though initially thankful to have herself escaped Lord Linley as a partner, Mary Anne would have gladly traded places with her sister when she saw the expression in the general's remarkable blue eyes as he watched the handsome couple. It was a long moment before he turned and left the drawing room. And though his face gave no indication of his feelings, Mary Anne, who stood nearby, did not believe she'd imagined he was troubled. Indeed, what with one thing and another, she concluded, there were quite enough currents abroad in the room to set one of the new electrifying machines into frantic action.

Captain Rodes had, of course, claimed the hand of his fiancée. He was leading her into the set just forming when she excused herself to speak to the Prussian who'd sat next to her at dinner. Lady Barbara then led him to the rows of chairs where Mary Anne and some other unpartnered ladies had retreated. "I'm acting as interpreter, Miss Hawtry. Count Roethke requests the honor of this dance."

Anthony appeared less than overjoyed when Mary Anne took her place beside him. He quickly turned his back, as if conversation with his betrothed demanded he lean toward her to put their heads quite close together. And when the movements of the dance required a change of partners, he gingerly took Mary Anne's fingertips in his gloved hand in much the manner that one might grasp a long-dead fish.

She retaliated with a firm grip and a vicious squeeze. "We need to talk," she hissed into his ear.

"We've nothing to talk about" was the stiff-lipped reply.

And in the intervals she and her Prussian partner strained their cheeks with fake smiles and tried to pantomime their delight in the exercise and in the music emanating from two violins, a bass viol, and a harp, performed upon an improvised platform banked with flowers.

At the conclusion of the set the Prussian thanked her, most likely with relief, then turned to engage Lady Barbara for the following dance. "Let's all have something to drink first," her ladyship replied, first in English, then in German, and led the way toward the refreshment table, with the Prussian at her heels.

"Pardon me," Captain Rodes said abruptly, "I must go do the proper and ask my hostess for a dance."

"In other words, even though your fiancée has more or

28

less thrown me at your head, you intend to leave me standing like a widgeon in the middle of the dance floor."

"It's a petty revenge, I grant you. Still, it may give you a minuscule notion of how I was made to feel."

"And did your father never point out that vengeance, petty or otherwise, is a sin?"

"He may have done. But then, I was always something of a disappointment to that saintly gentleman. Now if you'll excuse me." He bowed and left her.

Mary Anne had had quite enough. In case anyone, which she doubted, might wonder why she chose to desert the ballroom so soon, she began to fan herself vigorously to indicate she was overheated. Indeed the air was more pleasant in the hall. A quiet room with an open window would be even better. She could simply wait out the interminable evening and reappear when tea was served.

Cardplayers occupied the first drawing room she checked on, but the small blue parlor appeared deserted. She had sunk down thankfully in a wing chair and placed her satin evening slippers upon a cross stool before she realized her mistake. A murmur of voices came from one of the small balconies that dressed the first-floor windows overlooking the street. She might not quite catch all the words, but Mary Anne had no difficulty identifying the couple engaged in earnest conversation. It was her sister and Lord Linley Mortlock.

"I can't believe you'd hold a thing like that over my head." Sydney's voice rose in agitation. "No gentleman would do so."

"Ah, but then you've never really considered me a gentleman, now, have you? Indeed I've always suspected that fact was my chief attraction."

"What I never dreamed was that you'd deliberately wish to make trouble between my husband and myself. I still cannot credit it."

"Then perhaps your suspicions are misplaced."

"If that's so, pray return my property."

"*Your* property? What a convenient memory you have, m'dear. It's now my property. I won it, fair and square."

Mary Anne was ashamed to listen longer. She rose quietly from her chair and tiptoed to the doorway. She had eased it open and was on the point of fleeing when she spied her brother-in-law checking the rooms along the corridor. As Sir Maxwell paused in the entryway to the card room, Mary Anne softly reclosed the door, then sprinted back across the parlor to dash between the startled couple on the balcony.

"This air is famous. I vow I was simply perishing with the heat," Mary Anne remarked in a carrying voice as they heard the door click open. "I really think I might have swooned if you had not brought me here, Lord Linley. But there's no need for you to concern yourself any longer, Sydney. You should return to your guests." She was fanning herself vigorously and leaning weakly against the iron balcony when Sir Maxwell joined them.

"Here you are, m'dear. I'd wondered where you'd got to. Our guests are feeling neglected, I fear."

"Oh, I am sorry." Sydney's cool voice contained no echo of the impassioned interchange she'd just engaged in. "Mary Anne was feeling a bit faint. And I was concerned for her."

"So I just heard."

Mary Anne hoped she merely imagined a hint of dryness in his tone. After all, she did not really know her brother-in-law that well.

"Shall we leave your sister in Linley's care, then? My cousin is, I'm told, quite noted for his attentiveness to the fair sex."

"Oh, you can always rely on me, Maxwell." Smiling at his cousin all the while, his lordship relieved Miss Hawtry of her fan and began to ply it for her. "I can almost guarantee a speedy recovery," he prophesied.

"Undoubtedly." And with a polite bow for his relatives, Sir Maxwell offered his wife his arm and led her away.

"*Whoosh!*" As the door closed once more, Mary Anne expelled the breath she'd been holding. "And will you please stop waving that fan in front of my face, sir? Besides making me giddy, it's apt to bring on a case of the grippe."

"Pray do forgive me," the other purred. "You're such a consummate actress I'd almost forgot you aren't actually faint at all. But what you really are, of course, is a shocking little eavesdropper. Is that not so, m'dear?"

# Chapter
# Four

"Since we all had a late night, I expect I'll be the only one riding this morning," Mary Anne observed, a bit too casually, to the groom who was saddling a horse for her.

"Why, no, miss. As a matter of fact Captain Rodes left on Ajax just a bit ago."

This was the information she'd been digging for. Now she tried to hide her impatience with the groom's deliberateness. When she was at last mounted, she set off for the park at an unseemly gallop, too intent upon her mission to appreciate the treat of cool morning air and a cloudless sky.

Being all too familiar with Anthony's usual neck-or-nothing style, Mary Anne had almost despaired of catching him when she spied the large chestnut well ahead of her on Rotten Row. He was proceeding at a relatively sedate canter.

The park was almost deserted at this early hour. As she urged her own mount on, Mary Anne could have done with heavier traffic. She did not wish to arouse Anthony's curiosity about the rider overtaking him.

He did glance back, however, and spotted her. And as she'd feared, he immediately spurred his chestnut into a gallop. Mary Anne coaxed more speed out of her horse, but the mare was tiring fast. Then she saw Anthony glance again over his shoulder and actually slow down. Thankful for it, she murmured words of encouragement into her horse's ear. But as the gap between them began to narrow, the chestnut speeded up.

It soon became apparent he was playing cat and mouse, maintaining the same distance between them whether her mount flagged or surged ahead. Mary Anne herself rode well. She'd forgot he was a centaur. Little wonder he'd bought his colors in the cavalry. He'd had no choice.

He left the Row and turned off into a tree-lined path. She followed, thinking furiously. It was more than obvious he'd go to any length to avoid a tête-à-tête. Unless . . . She watched him duck low to avoid a tree branch growing across the path and quickly made up her mind. Breathing a prayer for deliverance, she grabbed the branch with both hands, held on, and let the horse ride out from under her.

Her scream was worthy of Mrs. Siddons. Except that the actress would have relied solely upon her art whereas Mary Anne miscalculated her descent and hit the ground with a teeth-rattling thump. The cry, once she'd recovered breath enough, reflected genuine anguish.

He wheeled and spurred back toward her. She was sitting in the path, fearing to move unless she couldn't, while her horse blissfully cropped grass a few yards ahead.

"You ninnyhammer!" Anthony was fuming as he dismounted. "Couldn't you see anything as large as a tree limb? You used to know how to ride."

He knelt beside her and began to run his hands over her

limbs to check for broken bones in a manner that might well have been called clinical except for its devastating effect upon Mary Anne.

"You might have waited for me," she said.

"I wished to ride alone."

"I didn't mean that. You might have waited on me before getting yourself betrothed."

He left off his examination to stare into her eyes with disbelief. "I must be examining the wrong areas. It's obvious now. You landed on your head."

"I did no such thing. And don't you dare walk away from me," she said hotly as he rose to his feet. "After all I've put myself through, we're going to talk."

He looked down in disgust. "You staged that fall, didn't you. I should have known."

"Thank you for coming back at least."

"I should not have done. And by God if you dare to limp when you stand up, I'll take both horses and ride out of here and you can walk home. There's nothing wrong with you."

Mary Anne was not quite so sure of that as she struggled unassisted to her feet. She suspected she'd be sitting on cushions for some time to come. "I really don't see why you're going to such lengths to avoid talking to me." Her tone was equally as injured.

"Because there's no point in it," he replied wearily. "As I recall, we said it all when I was last home on leave from the army. I asked you to marry me and you said no. That just about covered it, I'd say."

He walked over to retrieve his horse and she followed. "But you should have waited. You knew I'd change my mind."

"On the contrary, I didn't. You see, I'd no notion at all that I'd ever come into a fortune."

"Your fortune has nothing to say in the matter."

"Oh, does it not?" he sneered. "Is this Miss Mary Anne

Hawtry speaking? The same Miss Hawtry who assured me of her undying love but at the same time informed me she would never marry an impoverished soldier, but instead intended to barter her beauty to the highest bidder."

"I certainly never said an odious thing like that."

"Not in those precise words perhaps. But that was the general idea. I believe your actual stated ambition was to make as brilliant a match as Sydney had. So tell me, does your Lord Littlecote qualify?"

"He's not my Lord Littlecote any longer. But as a matter of fact he does—did." She couldn't resist hurling her triumph in his teeth, but she instantly regretted it as he tossed her none too gently into her saddle. "Ouch!" she protested.

"Anyhow," she continued as he walked toward his own horse, "all that has noting to say to anything. You knew me well enough to realize I didn't mean whatever it was I told you. You knew I'd not be able to get along without you. After all, I'd idolized you ever since I was old enough to tag along behind you. And certainly after you'd declared you'd always love me, too, I did not expect you to turn right around and get yourself engaged to the next female you met. It must have taken a lot of enterprise on your part amid all those battles. I really don't see how you ever found the time, much less the initiative. And they call women inconstent!" she sniffed.

He paused with one foot in the stirrup to turn and stare up at her. "My God, you're serious, aren't you? You turn down my offer of marriage with absolute finality. Your betrothal is announced in all the papers and yet you expect me to— languish!" He collapsed against his horse in helpless laughter.

"I don't see what's so amusing." She tossed her head haughtily. "I was only seventeen at the time and you knew how I was longing to make my come-out and enjoy a London Season."

"Well, you took the town by storm no doubt," he said dryly as he mounted up.

"As a matter of fact, I did. But after I'd got past all that and had actually landed Roderick, I knew I could not spend my life with him. It was unthinkable. I belonged with you."

"I can see your reasoning. Now that I'm a nabob." He clucked at his chestnut.

"Don't you dare run away from me again."

"I've no intention of it. I wouldn't miss a word of this. But after our gallop we shouldn't let our horses cool off too fast. We'll walk them back."

They proceeded in silence for a bit while she tried to collect her thoughts for a reasonable presentation of her case. "You really do believe it's only your fortune that has brought me back, don't you, Anthony?"

The look he shot her was eloquent.

"Very well, then. I deserve that. But just tell me one thing: Did Lady Barbara agree to marry you while you were still penniless?"

"I'd come into my fortune before Sir Maxwell introduced us" was the grudging answer.

So Maxwell had done the matchmaking. Her brother-in-law's stock was falling rapidly. "But you're convinced she'd still have said yes even though you were a pauper?"

"Certainly not."

"Well, then," she pounced like a debater who'd just made a telling point, "do you mind explaining why it's perfectly proper for Lady Barbara to be mercenary and not for me?"

"Because Lady Barbara had not pretended for donkey's years to love me, that's why."

"I was not pretending. But you always knew I was expected to marry a fortune."

"I should have done. Oh, I admit it. For I knew what you

36

were being schooled for. But I was sap-skulled enough to believe you were different from your sister."

"You never approved of Sydney, did you?" she accused.

"It depends upon how you mean that. I didn't approve of the way she looked down her beautiful nose at the rest of the world. But there was a time"—he grinned suddenly—"when I certainly lusted after her."

"Sydney doesn't look down her nose at the world—" Mary Anne had begun indignantly when she suddenly broke off. "What do you mean you *lusted* after her! That's a shocking thing to say!"

"Not in the least. At fifteen or whatever it's the most natural thing in the world, I'd say. All that toplofty beauty and her just enough older than myself to appear sophisticated. Of course I had my fantasies. Along with the rest of the male population of Hampshire, I've no doubt."

"Well, I must say I never suspected. I don't mean about the other males in Hampshire. I knew about them. But I actually thought you were the one exception. I was goosish enough to think you preferred me."

"Of course I preferred you. I never even liked her."

"Oh, no, of course not. You only *lusted* after her. That's an odious expression. Wherever did you get it?"

"It's biblical, I suppose. After all, I'm a clergyman's son, remember? And I didn't daydream through Papa's sermons the way you did. Now, could we drop the subject? God knows I regret introducing it."

"And well you should." Mary Anne was more than a bit miffed to learn of his carnal feelings for her sister and longed to inquire if he'd also lusted after her. But one look at his expression steered her onto a more prudent path.

"How is your papa?" she inquired politely.

"Quite well, thank you." He was just as formal. "He's now living in Surrey, as you may know."

37

"I do know. In fact I cried when he left the village. You may be surprised to learn it, but I loved your father. In spite of the fact that he never approved of me."

"My father was very fond of you."

"That's hardly the same, though I'm glad for it. I do know he was a lot more lenient with me than he was with you when he caught us kissing that time. Instead of telling Mama, he made me do 'penance,' as he called it, by teaching some of the poor village children to read. Which did my character no good at all since I rather enjoyed it. As I recall, he took a strap to you."

"Papa?" He chuckled, appearing for the moment to forget his enmity. "He never took a strap to Creighton or me in our entire lives, not that Creighton ever needed one. But no, he simply lectured me, that's all."

"On lust?"

"No! On the futility of falling in love with Mrs. Hawtry's daughter. There'd be no hope of a marriage between us, he told me. But of course I didn't believe him. Then."

"Well, that was hardly fair! I slaved all summer long and you only got a tongue-lashing. I suppose he considered the whole thing my fault."

"Not in the least," he said wearily. "He simply felt it would be a good thing for you to have the experience of doing something useful. And he was proud of the way you went about it. As I said, he quite liked you actually."

"I'm glad."

"But enough of the past. It's over. And we'd best get one thing clear." They were back on Rotten Row now and other early-morning equestrians were trotting by them. He reached out and took her bridle to pull them over to the side. "This sort of business has to stop here and now, Mary Anne. We'll have no more rendezvous. They're pointless. I'm betrothed. And if you aren't, you should be. You snared Littlecote once and can easily do so again. For God knows, you're even more beautiful now than I remembered, which makes you more than a match for any sap-skulled male. So let's just forget we ever knew each other.''

"Just like that.'' Her voice was disbelieving. "How am I supposed to forget a whole lifetime, pray tell?''

"By reminding yourself we're two different people now.''

"Yes,'' she answered slowly, trying to deal with the reality of his words. "At least in your case I collect it's true. You've been off to war and endured God knows what—for you're a hero, so they tell me.''

"That's fustian.''

"No, I'm sure you are one. It comes as no surprise. And you've inherited a fortune and are about to marry above your touch. Yes, I can see you're quite a different person. The problem is I'm still the same shallow widgeon I've always been.''

"Did I call you that? Well, then I beg pardon for it. But the only point worth making now is that we're not to see each other anymore.''

"That could be a bit difficult, staying in the same house and all.''

"You know damn well what I mean.'' He glared impatiently.

"Oh, yes, I know all right, Tell me one thing, Anthony. Would it make any difference if I told you that when I broke off my engagement to Lord Littlecote I'd no notion at all you'd come into a fortune?''

"Not the slightest.''

"Because you'd not believe me or because of Lady Barbara?''

"Both.'' They were emerging from the park, and he nudged his chestnut with his heel.

"Good-bye, Mary Anne. Consider this the parting of our ways."

"Oh, Anthony!" she called desperately after his retreating back. "There's just one more thing you should know."

"Yes?" He turned reluctantly.

"I hate your mustache!"

"Good!"

The succinct reply was not quite drowned out by the clatter of hooves on cobblestones.

# Chapter Five

"What are you doing here?" Mary Anne paused on the threshold of her bedchamber.

"Waiting for you, naturally. I had not expected you to be quite so energetic." As she sipped tea from a tray that had been meant for Mary Anne, Sydney's eyebrows rose as she took in her sister's riding habit. She was still in her dressing gown, propped against the pillows of the bed. "But I collect you had an ulterior motive for your early-morning exercise. I understand that Captain Anthony Rodes has been out riding, too."

Mary Anne refused to rise to bait, but removed her hat and gloves and gave the bellpull a tug. "And I had not expected you to be up and about so early. With your husband just home from the wars I should have thought—" She cut short what she was about to say and looked embarrassed.

"That we would have spent the morning in bed? Hardly.

Maxwell has business to attend to, or so his valet informed me.''

"His valet?''

"Indeed. The general slept in his dressing room, you see.''

"Oh, my heavens!'' Mary Anne sank down in a chair and stared at her sister. It was just as well that the maid arrived at that moment with a fresh pot of tea and a plate of scones.

"Sydney,'' Mary Anne blurted when the servant had gone, "you surely aren't saying that after such a long absence Maxwell didn't—hasn't—''

"Made love to me? No need to be so missish. No, I beg pardon. I'm the one who's being missish. I should not have described what transpired briefly between my husband and myself as 'making love.' And afterwards''—her voice was bitter—''he excused himself and retired to his dressing room. He did not wish to disturb my rest, you see. Or so he said. 'You've grown accustomed of course to sleeping alone' were his exact words.''

"Well, I expect he was merely trying to be considerate.'' Mary Anne tried to sound convincing.

"Or ironic perhaps.''

"Whatever do you mean?''

"Oh, nothing really. No doubt I misinterpreted his tone of voice.''

"Well, I should hold my tongue of course,'' Mary Anne began, then paused to search for the proper words.

"Am I to prepare myself for a scold?''

"In a way. I simply wish to point out that he's undoubtedly heard rumors that you and his odious cousin are thick as thieves. And if I had not been there with the two of you when Maxwell arrived on the balcony last night, well, he might have found some cause to spend the *entire* night in his dressing room.''

"Ah, yes, that. And I'm grateful to you, believe me. That's

why I'm here. To thank you for coming to the rescue. And to get your advice. I'm in a terrible coil, you see."

"Oh, surely you haven't fallen in love with that—loose fish!"

"In love with Linley? The notion's obscene. I loathe the man."

Mary Anne choked on the bite of scone she'd just taken. "Loathe him? I don't believe it. Why, you're always in his pocket. I even wondered if—"

"If he was my lover? You and the rest of the world, it appears. Well, you could not be more wrong if you thought that. Quite the opposite, in fact. One of Linley's chief attractions was that of all the gentlemen who dangled after me he was the only one who never tried to stray beyond the bounds of propriety. That, plus the fact that he was so amusing—at first, that is—*and* my husband's cousin made him the perfect escort.

"It's hard now to credit it, but when I first met Lord Linley I was so naive as to think he had only Maxwell's interests at heart. Now I know better. There's nothing he'd enjoy more than doing Maxwell a mischief. And from the moment we met, he deliberately set out to accomplish that through me. But then, you know all that. You overheard our conversation last night."

"Very little of it. I did hear that Lord Linley has something of yours you want, but he won't give it back. But that's all I heard."

"All?" Sydney forced a laugh. "Well, there you have the gist of it. Oh, Mary Anne, I'm in the worst coil of my life. And I've no notion at all what to do for the best. That's why I have to tell somebody about it."

Mary Anne looked at her sister in alarm. She'd never seen Sydney so distraught. Indeed, she'd rarely seen her fall prey to emotion of any kind. "What on earth does Lord Linley have of yours that can matter so much?"

"My portrait."

"Your portrait? Why would you ever give that tulip your portrait?"

"I didn't *give* it to him. He won it at cards."

"Oh, well then." Mary Anne shrugged dismissively. "People are always losing things at cards. That's nothing to make such a Cheltenham tragedy over."

"Don't be such a cloth-head!" her sister snapped. "Would I be making a Cheltenham tragedy, as you so tactfully put it, if it were a common, ordinary portrait?"

"How should I know if you don't go ahead and tell me what this is all about. Just how *extraordinary* is it?"

"It's nude."

The tea splashed out of Mary Anne's cup. "N-nude?"

"Well, almost so. I'm reclining on a couch—in the classical manner—and there is a bit of gauze draped here and there."

"How much exactly?"

"Just as I said. A bit."

"Oh, dear heavens!" Mary Anne stared, appalled, as her sister's color heightened.

"Well, really, Mary Anne, it hardly helps for you to take that attitude. I'd hoped for advice, not a preachment."

"I'm n-not about to preach," her sister protested. "I just can't imagine why you posed for such a thing, that's all. Much less," she choked, "how you came to stake it at cards."

"I posed for it because I planned to send it to Max. But then later on it seemed a stupid notion and so I didn't."

"Oh, well then." Mary Anne was recovering enough to wish to alleviate some of her sister's distress. "That doesn't

44

seem so very shocking. I suppose,'' she finished doubtfully, ''wives do that sort of thing all the time.''

''In point of fact it was a shatter-brained idea from the outset. But I'd wished to get his attention, you see. And it certainly would have done so.'' Sydney giggled suddenly, a bit hysterically. ''The thing measures three feet by five.''

''My word! I'm amazed you didn't just hire someone to paint you on his ceiling.''

''At the time I might have done if the idea had occurred.'' Sydney's smile was twisted. ''You see, I had just found out that Mrs. Edleston had moved to Portugal to be near Max.''

''And who, pray tell, is Mrs. Edleston?''

''You mean you don't know? Maxwell's mistress, of course.''

Tea drinking was providing altogether too perilous. Mary Anne had been in the process of replenishing her cup when her sister dropped this bombshell.

''I'm sorry.'' Sydney watched her carefully pour the contents of her saucer back into her cup. ''I hadn't meant to startle you. I just assumed the whole world knew of Mrs. Edleston.''

''Well, I certainly did not! Who is she anyhow? And are you sure she and Maxwell are—uh—?''

''Oh, yes, quite sure. They'd been lovers for years, you see, before he met and married me. Her husband was living then of course. The poor man's sense of timing was unfortunate, to say the least. He waited to pass on to his reward until Maxwell had become unavailable. Then, after a suitable mourning period''—her lip curled—''Mrs. Edleston pulled up stakes and went abroad to join the general. And that's when I hit upon the harebrained notion of reminding Maxwell why he married me. In part, at any rate.''

''But you don't actually believe he's in love with that— female—do you?''

"Certainly I believe it. Why, they've been together for donkey's years, except for occasional interruptions for weddings, funerals, and the like."

"And do you really mind?" Mary Anne was treading on delicate ground here, but her curiosity got the better of her judgement.

"Mind? Naturally, I mind. I'd love to scratch the doxy's eyes out!"

"Why, Sydney, you're actually jealous!" This surpassed belief.

"Of course I'm jealous. What would you expect?"

"But it's not as though you were actually in love with Sir Maxwell or anything like that."

"Oh, you think not?"

"You mean you actually are?" Mary Anne's mouth dropped open. "But I had supposed—"

"That I married Maxwell for his fortune? And to please Mama, who was throwing me at his head? Oh, I know that's what everybody thought. But the truth is, I fell hopelessly in love the moment I saw him. And I was determined to bring him up to scratch."

"But does Maxwell know how you feel about him?"

"Certainly not. He was obliged to marry to get an heir, don't you see, and was not looking to make a love match. I'm convinced my chief attraction was that it was well-known I'd come to the marriage mart to find a wealthy husband. Also I was the most decorative thing around. Oh, I do believe I quite turned his head in that respect.

"But then we were married and I became *enceinte* almost immediately and he only saw me casting up my accounts in the early days before he left to go back to the army. Then when he finally did get home just before Savannah was born, I was looking like a more than ordinarily awkward hippo."

"You were nothing of the sort. Don't be goosish. Everyone said you looked a perfect Madonna."

"Don't *you* be goosish. Anyhow, that's why I had the portrait painted. To remind him what he had waiting for him back home. But then later on I thought better of the whole maggoty idea."

"And staked the thing at cards." Mary Anne made no effort to keep the censure from her voice.

"That was not nearly so shocking as it now seems. For I'd no intention of ever parting with it of course."

"Does any gambler ever expect to lose?" The echoes of the Reverend Matthew Rodes were in Miss Hawtry's voice.

"Oh, I expected to lose all right." Sydney looked a trifle ill. "But I did not expect to have to forfeit.

"Now, of course, I know what a complete fool I was. You see, I'd told Linley about the painting. That was when I still thought of him as a friend. And now I realize what he intended all along. We'd always played cards together, you see, and I always lost. Linley's a nonesuch gamester you know, quite skillful and with Lucifer's own luck. We played for paltry stakes at first, and he always returned his winnings. It got to be a joke. He made a ceremony of tearing up my vouchers. And the stakes increased. I even lost the Cunliffe diamonds once."

Mary Anne gasped. "You didn't!"

"Oh, yes, I did. But he gallantly returned them. So when he suggested I stake the portrait, of course I agreed."

"In other words, you were diddled."

"Like the greenest flat. And now I know he'd been patiently working up to that all the time."

"But *why*?"

"God knows. Except that in some perverse way Linley sees it as a means of cutting Maxwell down to size. Oh, Mary Anne, he really hates his cousin. Don't ask my why. Perhaps he's envious of Maxwell's reputation. Or tired of having his cousin's military exploits flung in his teeth. All I know is when I asked him the same question he merely shrugged and said he thought it might be amusing to play Iago to Maxwell's Othello. Besides, he said, he'd always found the Shakespearean plot glaring weak in motivation. He thought a naked portrait could be a much more realistic instrument for jealousy than a mere wisp of handkerchief.''

"Surely he doesn't think Maxwell will strangle you. He's far more likely to call Lord Linley out.''

"Actually he won't do either. He doesn't care enough for me to be enraged. And he's far too fond of his aunt to put a bullet through her son's heart.''

"Then what? Surely Maxwell would not go through the scandal of a divorce?'' Her voice shook with horror at the notion. "Especially when you tell him the true circumstances.''

"And do you think he'd believe me? I'm well aware of what the gossip-mongers have been saying.

"But in answer to your question, no, I don't think for a minute that Maxwell would drag the family name through the mud of divorce.'' For just a moment, though, Sydney looked frightened. "Not unless he's head over heels in love with Mrs. Edleston, that is, and wants his freedom for her sake.''

"I'm sure he'd never do anything so—unthinkable,'' Mary Anne said stoutly. "So even if the worst does happen, it won't be the end of the world, now, will it?''

"It will be the end of my world.'' Tears formed in her eyes. "For if my husband believes I posed naked for a painting intended for his cousin, I'm confident he'll have no more to do with me. Perhaps you're not aware of it, but Maxwell is an extremely proud man.''

48

"Well, his pot would have no right to call your kettle black! Mrs. Edleston indeed!"

"You know better than that, Mary Anne. A man may do just as he chooses. But a woman must at all times be discreet. And Linley intends to insure I appear anything but that." Her voice broke. "Oh, Mary Anne, what am I to do?"

"Have you appealed to Lord Linley's better nature?"

"He doesn't have one."

"You've offered to buy if back?"

"Don't be a sap-skull. Of course I've done so."

"Well, then, there seems to be just one avenue left open to us."

"And that is?"

"Why, we'll simply have to steal the painting, won't we?"

# Chapter
# Six

"And just how are we expected to steal the painting?"
Sydney surveyed her sister with disgust. "Even if we could get at the cursed thing, have you forgot its dimensions? You'd hardly stick a thing that size in your reticule."

"Well, you can't expect me to have worked out any of the details," Mary Anne snapped back. "After all, I've just learned of the wretched portrait's existence. But I do know this much . . ."—she brightened up a bit—"if you're going to steal a painting, you never bother with the frame. You simply cut out the canvas and roll it up. And while that still might not fit into a reticule, it should not be all that difficult to conceal. And come to think on it, it really isn't necessary to steal the thing. Destroying it would be sufficient. For I should think you would be glad enough to get rid of it."

"Well, after all it is a work of art."

"Sydney! This is no time for aesthetic consideration. Ripping the thing up or painting over it may turn out to be the thing to do."

"Oh, for heaven's sake, will you stop it! This conversation is too ridiculous. We aren't going to be able to do any of those things. We've got to find someone to help us."

"Oh, well now. *That* suggestion's not at all ridiculous." Mary Anne's voice oozed sarcasm. "Why don't you just order one of the servants to steal it?"

"I was thinking more of Anthony."

"Anthony!"

"Sssh! Keep your voice down. Can you think of a more likely person? He's resourceful—and daring—and—"

"Honorable?"

"And a man would have easy access to Linley's rooms, whereas we would not. And once there, he could possibly find the thing and rip it up or something."

"And then be hauled off to Newgate?"

"Oh, don't look at me like that. I'm well aware I'm grasping at straws. But could you at least speak to him about it?"

"I don't see how, for he doesn't wish ever to speak to me again, actually. You see, he—"

Here they were interrupted by a tap on the door. A maid entered.

"There's a gentleman downstairs to see Miss Hawtry, your ladyship. Lord Littlecote's 'is name. Mr. Carson's put him in the library." She looked from one lady to another.

"Oh, no, Roderick!" Mary Anne groaned. "It needed only this. Could I not send word I'll not see him?"

"Don't be goosish. Of course you'll see him. This may be the only stroke of luck likely to come our way. At least one of us may get a second chance. So run on and try to make amends. Say you were suffering from a temporary bout of brain fever when you broke the engagement. Or something of the sort. Now go!"

It would be nice, Mary Anne thought as she entered the library, if just for once a gentleman's face were to light up when she walked into a room. She was not even certain she preferred Roderick's reproach above Anthony's scorn.

Lord Littlecote had been pacing up and down. He now paused to fix her with a stare.

Mary Anne gazed back warily, hardly knowing just what tack to take. The uppermost thought in her mind was: What a pity I can't love him. Why could she not have been like Sydney and tumbled head over heels for her wealthy conquest? For really, Roderick was not at all bad to look at. His light brown hair was modishly swept into a Brutus. His features, while not prepossessing perhaps, did well enough. True, his figure might run to stoutness before long, but the exquisite cut of his Bond Street tailoring minimized this tendency. The problem was, simply stated, she found him tedious to the extreme. But then perhaps tediousness was not the greatest fault to be found in a husband. Mary Anne dismissed these thoughts since they could not very well go on staring at each other forever. "What on earth brings you to London, Roderick?" she asked.

"Now, I'd call that a damn fool question, I would!"

The reply caused Mary Anne's eyes to widen. It was totally unlike Roderick to explode, much less to swear.

"What did you expect me to do, for God's sake, after you'd run off without a word except the cursed note you left for me?"

Well, really she had not given the matter a great deal of thought. "Why nothing, actually."

"Nothing!" He was quivering with anger. "A cove gets a letter saying the woman he's betrothed to loves another, and he's supposed to just go on about his business as though nothing at all had happened? Now, I ask you!"

"Please, Roderick, do keep your voice down." Mary Anne glanced nervously over her shoulder in case any other members of the household were in earshot. She thought it prudent to go close the door.

"Now, then," she said in the same soothing tone she might take with Savannah. "Why don't we sit down and talk this over calmly? Would you like me to ring for tea?"

"No" was the sullen reply. But he did allow himself to be steered to a settee. Mary Anne sat down beside him. "Brandy, perhaps?"

"No, dammit! Will you quit acting as though I'm simply here to pay a morning call and explain yourself, miss!"

"There's no need to keep shouting at me. I'm not deaf, you know." Mary Anne was growing a trifle nettled. "And I can't explain myself. At least no better than I did in the note I left you. I just decided we wouldn't suit, that's all."

"It's not *all*, by God. You said there was some other cove involved, dammit, and I demand to know just who the fellow is."

"Well, you needn't demand it, for I'm not about to tell you. And actually he has nothing to say in the matter."

"Nothing to say in the matter! By George, Mary Anne, that is rich, that is. A dog in the manger steals a cove's fiancée and the widgeon is supposed to just blink at it? Well, it ain't my style, I'll assure you. If you won't tell me, then I'll find out on my own, by God."

Mary Anne was growing quite alarmed. This was a side of the prosish Lord Littlecote she'd never suspected. "Really, Roderick, you are being absurd. Actually there isn't anyone else. I just thought I needed to furnish a better reason than the honest truth, which is that we simply will not suit. And frankly, Roderick, I rather suspected you'd be relieved."

"Relieved! Relieved! To be made a monkey of! A laughingstock! My God, woman, what will everyone say? Our engagement's been *announced*, for God's sake. Printed in the *Gazette*."

"Well, the *Gazette* is hardly holy writ," she pointed out reasonably. "We'll not be the first couple to cry off. And as for you becoming a laughingstock, why, that's ridiculous. I expect the truth of the matter will be that most folk will think you've come to your senses. I know your mother must be quite relieved."

"No, she ain't."

"Well, that does amaze me. I was sure she didn't like me above half."

"She don't. But she can't be relieved, can she, for I've not told her what's what. I certainly ain't about to let her know you've thrown me over. Did you think I'd want to put up with all those 'I told you so's?"

"Then how on earth did you explain my disappearance?"

"I said you'd had an urgent letter from your sister, that Lady Cunliffe was unwell and needed you to help her entertain her guests."

"And your mother believed it?"

"Naturally. Oh she thought it rag-mannered of you, right enough, to go off early in the morning without doing the polite. But then she said it was only to be expected and the price she had to pay for having a son who didn't realize his own consequence and was bound and determined to marry beneath his touch.

"But actually, she didn't object at all when I said I planned to come to the metropolis to join you." Upon reflection he sounded more than a bit surprised. "When it comes right down to it," he mused further, "while she don't like the notion of me marrying a dowerless female, she does like the fact that you're connected to Sir Maxwell Cunliffe. Especially now that the whole country's gone wild over Bonaparte's defeat, and are calling Sir Maxwell one of England's heroes. So Mama did say that it wouldn't hurt my consequence to spend a fortnight or so under Sir Maxwell's roof and that I just might meet the crème de la crème of international society. The Czar of Russia! The King of Prussia!'' His expression had changed from injured to animated. ''As Sir Maxwell's guests we're bound to be included in all the celebration. Why, I'll bet a monkey we're even asked to Carlton House.''

''But you can't possibly stay here.''

''Where else do you expect me to stay? Told you I'd leased my house to a bunch of Russians, didn't I?''

''But it's unthinkable now that you and I are no longer—'' she broke off as the library door opened.

''Oh, I do beg your pardon.'' Lady Barbara seemed instantly aware that she'd intruded on a tête-à-tête. ''I didn't realize there was anyone in here. I wished to return a book I'd borrowed. Pray don't let me interrupt you.''

''Oh, but you aren't. Not a bit of it.'' Mary Anne managed to dredge up a polite smile. ''Do allow me to present Lord Littlecote. He's just come from Bath. And this is Lady Barbara Kennet, Lord Littlecote. She traveled from the Continent in Sir Maxwell's party.''

''Why, yes, I know, actually.'' His lordship was beaming. ''My mother and I had heard as much. And she was particularly eager that I make your acquaintance, Lady Barbara, so that I might convey her greetings to you and through you to your mother. They were particularly good friends as girls, it seems. At boarding school together. My mama was the former Miss Catherine Claridge. Perhaps your mother spoke of her?''

''Would that be Kitty Claridge? Well, indeed she did! Why, they were bosom bows. Mama will be delighted that I've met her friend's son, Lord Littlecote. I must write and say so right away. Perhaps your mother doesn't know that Mama is in Vienna. My father is in the foreign service and has been posted there to help prepare for the congress.''

"That will be news to her. Thought you lived in Spain. Well, well, well now. My mother will be more than pleased that I've met you."

"Err—ah—would you pray excuse me for just a moment?" During the exchange Mary Anne's head had been turning from one young person to the other, for all the world like a spectator at a tennis match. Now that she'd interrupted the flow she went on to say, "Why don't you two catch up on your mothers' histories while I go inform my sister that Lord Littlecote will be staying with us for a while. I'm sure she'll be in raptures, Roderick.

"Oh, Lady Barbara, if you don't mind, would you ring for tea? I'll only be a moment. In the meantime you two carry on." There was a cat-who'd-been-in-the-cream look on Miss Hawtry's face as she began a deliberately long and drawn-out search for Lady Cunliffe.

Then, when finally informed of this latest addition to her household, Sydney had merely shrugged. "Why not? Lord Littlecote is all that's needed. So far we have two German-speaking diplomats who can only smile and bow at the rest of us; a pair of lovebirds, one of whom spends his time glaring daggers at his former sweetheart; a lionized hero who, when he cannot avoid his wife altogether, is as studiously polite as he might be to a stranger. Then there are the two Hawtry beauties who have managed to muck up their lives to a degree requiring some sort of destructive genius. So to spice up the mix we could certainly use a fire-breathing, spurned, and jilted fiancé. By all means, let us welcome Lord Littlecote with open arms."

# Chapter
# Seven

*S*ydney's *description of their ill-assorted group was up-*
permost in Mary Anne's mind the following morning as
she drank a cup of restorative tea in bed. Certainly the house
party had appeared in the worst possible light when they'd
dined *en famille* the night before. Well, there had been one
exception.

It was Lady Barbara Kennet who had risen to the occasion
when Sydney, usually the most skillful of hostesses, seemed
to have lost all sense of obligation to her guests and merely
toyed with her food in silence while stealing occasional
glances at her equally mute husband.

Mary Anne had previously made one feeble attempt to
lighten the atmosphere. But since she'd ill-advisedly addressed her remark to Anthony and received a monosyllabic
answer for her pains, she'd quickly dropped the notion of
playing hostess.

Lady Barbara had then stepped into the breach to draw out Lord Littlecote on the English sport of fox hunting, which she managed to translate softly for the Prussians while scarcely interrupting Littlecote's flow. Even her fiancé managed to unbend a bit when she questioned him upon the subject. Then, under subtle probing, Sir Maxwell was awakened to his duty and shared some of his experiences with the Quorn.

Yes, there could be no question about it, Anthony was making a brilliant match. Lady Barbara was not only wealthy and personable, she was the epitome of all a lady should be, a product of good breeding coupled with a genuine regard for the feelings of those around her.

These reflections had plunged Mary Anne into the deepest gloom. It was positively the outside of enough to be forced to admire your beloved's fiancée. She therefore welcomed the distraction when her chamber door burst open and a tiny nightcapped whirlwind swept inside. ''Wanna go feed ducks!'' Miss Savannah Cunliffe announced.

''Indeed? Well then, why not? Sounds like a perfectly famous idea to me. Only no more 'pity shoes,' all right? Tell Becky to dress you in your scruffiest clothes.''

A little later the aunt and niece, attired in their oldest walking dresses, came up from the kitchen regions just as Lady Barbara, Captain Rodes, Lord Littlecotes, and Sir Maxwell were emerging from the breakfast parlor.

''Go feed ducks,'' Savannah informed the group with gracious civility as she held aloft the bag of stale bread she'd just acquired. She then turned her large blue eyes upon her father and studied him for a moment in solemn concentration. This inspection concluded with an approving smile that, except for her tender years, might have been called coquettish.

''My God, would you look at that,'' Anthony breathed.

"I'll swear it's in the blood. Here's another generation of Hawtry heartbreakers."

"She's not a Hawtry!" Mary Anne snapped. "Savannah is a Cunliffe."

"Well, you can hardly deny she's the very image of—her mother."

"She looks a great deal like Miss Hawtry here to my way of thinking," Lord Littlecote chimed in, looking back and forth between the aunt and niece judiciously. "Can imagine you were very much like that at her age, Mary Anne."

"Well, she may look like Sydney and me, but she isn't like us in the least." Mary Anne was not sure herself why she was contesting the alleged resemblance so hotly. "She's very much a Cunliffe. She's bright and knows her own mind already. And when she's older, she can afford to be independent and will have no need to—" She stopped, appalled at what she was about to say.

"No need to dangle after a fortune?" Savannah's father spoke lightly, though his eyes were hard. "You are quite right, you know. I intend to see that Savannah marries as she chooses."

"Oh, but I didn't mean—" Mary Anne's face had flamed. "You surely cannot think—" She was ready to sink. Sir Maxwell had no way of knowing she was comparing Savannah to herself, not to Sydney. Lord Littlecote, however, seemed to take her point. He was glaring daggers at her.

"We all know exactly what you mean," Anthony volunteered. "You're merely making the point that this little tot is brighter than you are. And as the one who's known you longest, I can vouch for that."

"What a horrid thing to say!" Lady Barbara gave her fiancé a distressed look. "Miss Hawtry may not realize you're funning."

"Pay no attention." Sir Maxwell forced a chuckle. "You

may not be aware, Lady Barbara, that Anthony grew up next door to my wife and Mary Anne. His father was their vicar. They were like brother and sisters, so Sydney tells me. *Squabbling* brother and sisters, I might add."

"Go feed ducks!" Savannah had had her fill of adult chatter. She tugged at Mary Anne's hand.

"Hold on a bit, little one," her father smiled. "I was about to suggest that some of the rest of us might like to join you. Lady Barbara, I fear that my wife has the headache this morning and will not be able to entertain you. Have you visited our park?"

"Not since I was a little girl myself and fed the ducks. I should love the exercise. will you not come too, Anthony? And you, Lord Littlecote?"

Lord Littlecote assured them with a heartiness that smacked more of civility then sincerity that there was nothing he'd enjoy half so well as making the acquaintance of the Hyde Park ducks.

Mary Anne was sufficiently recovered from her recent embarrassment to realize this could be an opportunity to further his lordship's friendship with Lady Barbara if only she were unimpeded by a fiancé. She turned an ingenuous face toward her 'brother.' "Oh, I've just remembered, Captain Rodes, that O'Toole wants your opinion of the mare Sydney's thinking of buying. He was hoping you'd go with him to Tattersall's this morning.

"O'Toole was our groom in Hampshire," she explained to Lady Barbara and Lord Littlecote. "He was one of the servants Sydney brought to London with her. He considers Anthony here the last word when it come to horseflesh."

"The devil he does." Anthony's look seemed to see right through her. "The day Ryan O'Toole listens to anybody else's opinion about his cattle, let alone mine, is the day pigs sprout wings. Let's go find those ducks."

They left Cunliffe House with Savannah clinging to Mary Anne with one hand and clutching her bag of bread crumbs with the other. Sir Maxwell fell in step beside them while the other three walked on ahead. "She's very fond of you," he observed during a lull in his small daughter's stream of chatter, which was largely unintelligible but appeared to deal mostly with ducks and gingerbread.

"I'm fond of her, too." Mary Anne beamed down at her niece's chip-straw bonnet.

"That's quite evident. You devote a lot of time to her, do you not?"

"Well, yes. And so does Sydney as a general thing, you know. You mustn't think these last few days are typical. It's just that she's been too involved with guests and all to spend much time with Savannah. And of course she's not feeling quite top of the trees either. But Sydney's wonderful with the child." She looked up earnestly at the general. "I would certainly not have expected her to take to motherhood the way she has. But she's really quite marvelous. Not at all like our mother. And Savannah adores her."

"There's really no need to defend Sydney to me." Sir Maxwell spoke dryly. "I happen to be well aware that my wife is a devoted mother. As a matter of fact I make it my business to know a great deal about my household in my absence."

Since Mary Anne found this remark rather unsettling, she was just as glad that her niece's decision to sit down suddenly in the middle of Rotten Row made it unnecessary to reply.

"Me tired," the little one announced.

Her father stooped obligingly and Savannah climbed upon his back. "Want to gallop?" he inquired, and proceeded to do so while his daughter, her wrists firmly clasped in his large hands, her white-stockinged legs wrapped around him as far as they would go, crowed with jolted laughter.

Mary Anne ran beside them till they caught up with the others. She gratefully slowed down then to a more sedate pace while they all watched the prancing hero of Vitoria. It was Captain Rodes who put into words what the rest of them were thinking. "I'd give a monkey if the regiment could see what I'm seeing now." He chuckled. "Do you know they call him Stoneface because he never shows any emotion, no matter how rough things get?"

The "horse" was galloping in circles now, as the squeals grew louder. "Sydney thinks he was deeply disappointed when he had a daughter," Mary Anne observed.

"Fustian."

"Well, of course, Rodes, a chap does need an heir," Lord Littlecote said thoughtfully. "True, it don't have to be the first arrow in the quiver, but a male child's bound to be a relief, don't you know."

Nobody challenged this truism.

Mary Anne's thoughts were on here sister's more pressing problems. How tragic if Lord Linley's maliciousness should come between Sir Maxwell and his family. For surely if the general could come to love his daughter as dearly as he obviously did, it would be a small step indeed to include the mother in that affection. Especially a mother with all the natural endowments Sydney was blessed with.

The path had narrowed. She and Anthony fell behind the other two who were in earnest conversation.

"Must be a relief not to have those Prussian coves dangling after you," Lord Littlecote was saying. "Can't for the life of me see what business they have coming over here when they can't speak a word of the tongue."

"Oh, come now, you are hard, sir." Lady Barbara laughed up at him. "It's only natural that the Prussian people are as eager as we English to take part in the peace celebration. It was a joint victory, after all."

Lord Littlecote's sniff conveyed how little he agreed. "Don't expect you chaps got all that much help from a bunch of foreigners, did you, Rodes?" he commented over his shoulder. "Or ever wanted it, I'll vow."

But before the captain could reply, he reverted to the initial point he'd been making. "Still think they've no cursed business coming over here if they can't speak properly."

"But, Lord Littlecote," Lady Barbara protested good-humoredly, "you would be amazed at how many English travel abroad without knowing one word of the host country's language."

"Well, that ain't the same thing at all, now, is it?"

"Oh, you really are droll, sir." Her ladyship gurgled with laughter. His lordship reacted to its infectiousness with a broad, if slightly puzzled, smile.

They had reached the serpentine, and the adults watched with amused pleasure as Savannah reached into her bag and began to scatter crumbs with earnest concentration. She was soon surrounded by a quacking, scrapping feathered mob. He father stepped into the circle to stand protectively by the tot lest quick bills snapped the tiny fingers before they could loose their bread.

"Oh, look, there's a magpie!" Lady Barbara exclaimed as a black-and-white bird insinuated itself among the larger fowl and jostled for its share of bread crumbs. "This is the first I've seen since I've been back in England."

"Oh, heavens, it's bad luck to see *one* magpie!" Mary Anne exclaimed. "I wonder where its mate is. You have to see 'two for joy,' you know."

"Surely you don't believe that nonsense," scoffed Lord Littlecote.

"Certainly, she does," Captain Rodes said. "And just ask her about black cats. Your fiancée's a regular gypsy when it comes to superstition."

"Goodness, you two do know each other well." Lady Barbara's tone was light, but here eyes were thoughtful.

When the attention focused upon Savannah and her flock once more, Mary Anne, who'd been wondering if this was the time and place to try and have a word with Anthony, threw caution to the wind and clutched his sleeve. "Do you remember when you stole the apple for me?"

He looked as though she'd suddenly taken leave of her senses. "Why bring that up just now? But of course I remember. Old Hicks took a potshot at me and damned near killed me."

"Oh, I don't think he really meant to hit you."

"No, he was right on target. He hit the limb I was clinging to, which came crashing down with me."

She giggled at the memory. "But you held on to the apple through it all."

He grinned, too, then seemed to recall himself. "Look, I told you this before. I'm not interested in reviving our past history."

"But this doesn't have anything to do with us." She tugged him a bit farther apart from the group. "Well, it does in a way, of course, but that's not the point. The point is, do you remember *why* you stole it?"

"You wanted it. My God . . ."—he looked disgusted— "you were merely six and I was all of nine, but it was real Garden of Eden stuff just the same."

"Oh, for heaven's sake, can't you forget for a moment that you're a vicar's son? You went after the apple because we'd gone into the woods and got lost and then we'd walked and walked and I thought we'd never get out. And then when we did I fell down the ditch and hurt myself and cried, partly because of the fall but mostly because I was tired and hungry."

"You were a pain."

64

"But the point is, you did something you would not ordinarily dream of doing because it seemed more right to you to do so than not doing it would seem."

"Just what the devil are you getting at with all this 'end justifies the means' drivel?" He glared at her suspiciously. "You're up to something, aren't you? My God, I'd forgot how conniving you can be. What's this all about, Mary Anne?"

"I'm simply trying to remind you that though the notion of stealing something might seem reprehensible and unthinkable at first blush, there are, after all, circumstances when thievery might be necessary—indeed, moral."

"I doubt my father would subscribe to your liberal notions. But come on. Out with it. Just what's your point?"

"Oh, I say, are you two talking of all the thievery that's going on around here?" Lord Littlecote had pricked up his ears. He now edged nearer to join the conversation. "That's a dashed good notion. And, Lady Barbara, you should get in on it. You people who are new to the metropolis can't have any proper notion of the amount of crime here. Especially thievery. London's a regular mecca for cutpurses. And with the town so crowded for the celebration, well, it's bound to get worse and worse. So you ladies keep a tight grip on your reticules. That's my advice."

"Well, I'd heard of course," Lady Barbara, who had obediently joined them, observed, "that there was a great deal of crime in London. But I thought it was largely confined to the dock areas, places like that."

"Oh, lord, no. Well, murder and the like are worse there of course," Littlecote conceded. "But when it comes to purse snatching and housebreaking, the villains come here to the West End where the pickings are better."

"Housebreaking?" Mary Anne's eyes had widened.

"Oh, my, yes." Lord Littlecote expanded under such rapt

65

attention. "Sir Geoffrey Carswell's house in St. James's Square was robbed just before I left for Bath this last time. Took everything but the furniture, by gad, or close enough. That's why I let out my own place. Don't do to leave one standing empty. Open invitation to the professionals."

"*Professional* thieves?" Mary Anne breathed. "I hadn't thought of such."

"Well, you should do," Lord Littlecote said indulgently. "And I'd warn Lady Cunliffe about 'em if I was you."

"Gracious, you'll have us all in a quake." Lady Barbara shivered. "I had thought with Bow Street so near the problem wouldn't exist."

"Bow Street helps some, I collect. But they can only do so much, shorthanded as they are. The problem is, you see, that your thief can rob somebody around here and then it's only a skip and a jump over to Drury Lane or Tothill Fields or one of the other thieves' kitchens. Your criminal can be swallowed up in no time."

"You're saying, then," Mary Anne asked, "that any thief who's worth his salt—a professional, in other words—is apt to get away with his crime?"

Captain Rodes watched her suspiciously while Lord Littlecote proceeded to expound upon her question.

"Almost bound to. Oh, some folk hire their own thief takers from Bow Street, don't you know. And sometimes those coves do manage to bring the rascals in. But if your thief makes it back to one of the rookeries where the neighborhood's bound and determined to hide him, he's safe as houses and no mistake. Actually, the chances of your thief getting away with his crime are about ninety-nine out of a hundred, I'd say."

"That good? My, but it really does make one stop and think."

Mary Anne was unusually quiet as they turned for home.

It was a good thing Savannah kept up a constant stream of chatter that held her father's fascinated attention and that Lord Littlecote had taken it upon himself to entertain Lady Barbara with his knowledge of the current London scene, for that only left Captain Rodes unaccounted for and she didn't give two figs about his silence. She was far too preoccupied to bother doing the polite with Anthony, who would snub all attempts at conversation anyhow.

But he perversely started one himself. "Why all this sudden interest in thievery?" he asked abruptly.

"*I'm* not interested in it. It was Roderick who brought up the subject."

"I beg to differ. Littlecote only chimed in after you'd been speaking of pilfered apples and philosophizing over when it was right or wrong to take something that doesn't belong to you. Out with it, Mary Anne. What the devil are you up to?"

"Up to? I'm not up to anything. How ridiculous you are."

"I wish I could believe that. The problem is, I know you too well." He frowned as her gaze darted here and there over the landscape. "For instance, I know when you won't look a person in the eye, it means you're up to no good."

"It does not! It simply means that I'm hunting for my second magpie. Oh, look there's one!" A bird took off in a whir of feathers from the upper branches of a tall oak tree.

"That's no magpie, you little pea-goose. That's a pigeon."

"Oh."

Ah, well, what did it matter. The others were right. It was sap-skulled to believe that a solitary magpie was an evil omen. Mary Anne was certainly not going to take the thing seriously. But she shivered nonetheless.

# Chapter Eight

*I*t was a tribute to the consequence of Sir Maxwell Cunliffe that he'd been able to obtain a box at Covent Garden. *The Grand Alliance*, an allegory composed especially for the peace celebration to compliment London's foreign visitors, was being performed that evening. The theater was packed to overflowing.

As the Cunliffe party took their places, cheers arose from the gallery. "My word, just wait till Mama hears of this," Lord Littlecote crowed in Mary Anne's ear.

"You do realize they're cheering for Sir Maxwell and not for the rest of us," she retorted, then instantly felt ashamed. Why shouldn't Roderick bask in the reflected glory if he wished to? Just because her own problems kept her from appreciating the occasion was no reason to spoil his pleasure in it. "Oh, look, there's Prinny!" she said by way of atonement, nodding toward the royal box. She pulled an opera glass from the recesses of her reticule and handed it to him with a smile.

"Oh, by Jove!" His lordship trained the glass upon the corpulent crown prince who was more than usually resplendent in one of his specially designed uniforms. "Those two coves with him must be the Czar and King Frederick, but deuced if I can tell which is which. Both look foreign, don't you know."

"The one with the mustache is the King of Prussia. At least I think so," Mary Anne replied doubtfully. Indeed, had it not been for all the gold braid, the medals, and the epaulets, all three of the royal gentlemen would have proved disappointingly ordinary.

The same could not be said of their party, she thought complacently. There was no more attractive couple in the house than Sir Maxwell and Lady Cunliffe. The general wore his uniform with an ease that made the royals appear to be in fancy dress. And while not precisely handsome, he possessed an air of distinction that made handsomeness commonplace. Then Sydney, her sister decided, had never looked more beautiful. She was dressed rather simply in an Urling's net round dress over a white satin slip. Her only jewelry was a choker of small diamonds about her lovely throat. This understated ensemble enhanced her natural beauty and defied the fashionable excesses of the majority.

Well, the rest of us needn't put our host and hostess to the blush, Mary Anne thought as she ran an approving eye over their party. She refused, however, to dwell on Anthony's appearance. It was really most unfair to give him the added dash of a dress uniform. Anthony in any guise had always set her pulses racing. Better to concentrate upon the Prussians, both of whom had managed to look most heroic though the significance of their uniforms was as mysterious as that of the Crown Prince's.

Lord Littlecote was the only male member of their party in civilian evening dress, a magpie among peacocks. But his coat had the unmistakable cut of the finest Bond Street tailoring. "Weston," he'd said with pride when she'd complimented him upon it. His starched shirt points were so high and stiff as to make turning his head an impossibility. Nor could even the great Beau Brummell have found fault with the perfection of his cravat. In fact, Roderick looked as nice as she'd ever seen him, and she herself was passable in a new gown of pale blue gros de Naples. While he and she might not measure up to her sister and brother-in-law's elegance, they looked well enough together, she supposed. The thought was somehow lowering. Perhaps because thinking of couples forced her attention back on Anthony and his fiancée.

Lady Barbara's eyes were sparkling as she laid a gloved hand on her escort's sleeve. She wore white lace over a pale rose-colored satin and for a headdress, a tall white satin toque. Like Lord Littlecote, she had never appeared to better advantage. "Oh this is just like being in fairyland!" she exclaimed, and her fiancé smiled at her enthusiasm.

Indeed Covent Garden deserved the comparison. It was all aglow. The occasion had demanded of everyone the optimum in finery. Silks, satins, and taffetas lent their multicolored luster to the scene. The flames of myriad candles danced off the crystal prisms of the enormous chandeliers. Quizzing and opera glasses flashed back their beams. Jewels sparkled as plumed heads turned to greet their friends or bent to whisper comments in companions' ears.

Mary Anne retrieved her glass from Roderick and slowly scanned the theater, drinking in the scene. As she swept the horseshoe of boxes, it was more than a bit disconcerting to shortly focus upon the magnified image of Lord Linley Mortlock and find him quizzing her. She did not dignify his mocking smile with any acknowledgment. Nor did she pause to note the other members of his party.

The orchestra played ''God Save the King,'' and the packed house rose to its feet. Mary Anne joined in the singing, and as she did so, turned, like most, to watch the royal box. The surge of pride she felt as her eyes rested upon the Regent failed to strike her as inappropriate. Prinny might often appear a figure of ridicule, but upon occasions like this, the celebration of England's triumph over her longtime foe, the Prince of Wales shone at his royal best. His subjects might hiss and boo him at other times, and with just cause, but now those packed into Covent Garden could look at him affectionately and include him, along with poor mad King George, in their musical petition for a saving grace.

The moment was, alas, short-lived. No sooner had the last patriotic note been wafted away and the prince and the royal sovereigns resumed their seats than a shout rose from the audience, followed by a spontaneous outbreak of applause.

''Heaven help us, it's Caroline!'' Sydney breathed, reaching over to clutch her sister's hand and draw her attention to the box now being entered by some latecomers. Mary Anne snatched up the glass once more and aimed it at the notorious Princess of Wales.

It focused upon a rather dumpy lady wearing a black wig and far too many diamonds. Mary Anne found the princess a disappointment. Really, she looked quite ordinary. But then, she would have needed to sprout a second head to live up to her royal reputation for eccentricity.

''What's all the fuss about?'' Lord Littlecote squinted toward the object of so much attention. ''Can't see a thing. You'd think they'd not be so stingy with their candles.''

He was known to be quite sensitive about his shortsightedness, so Mary Anne tactfully refrained from comment as she handed the opera glass to him.

"Humph!" was his lordship's only pronouncement upon the princess. It summed up the situation very well.

Everyone in the theater knew that the presence of his consort was a bitter pill for the Crown Prince to swallow. Throughout the celebration he had done his utmost to keep his estranged wife away from the foreign visitors. This had not been easy. The Czar and his rag-mannered sister, the Grand Duchess Catherine of Oldenburg, had often and pointedly inquired after Her Royal Highness. So now Prince George must have been silently cursing his wife as the audience, by necessity if not by choice, turned its back upon him to applaud the princess. The Czar and King Frederick both rose and bowed. The Prince had little choice but to follow suit.

After this, anything that took place on stage could only be an anticlimax. But when the pandemonium at last died down a bit the orchestra did its valiant best to redirect attention, and the curtain rose. The fictitious marshals of England, Russia, Prussia, Holland, France, Sweden, Germany, and Spain took their places and earnestly began to enact *The Grand Alliance.*

Mary Anne's mind could not focus upon the pageantry. She was trying to think of a way to gain a private word with Lord Linley Mortlock. Unappealing as that prospect was, she felt it necessary. Before she embarked upon the foul means she had in mind to get back her sister's portrait, it seemed only sensible to make certain it could not be obtained by fair. Perhaps Sydney had misinterpreted his lordship's intentions. Or perhaps he himself had had second thoughts. At any rate she felt compelled to feel him out upon the subject before plunging into the murky waters of criminality.

All her stewing proved to be a waste of time, however. The mountain came to Muhammad, as it were. Lord Linley visited their box at the first interval. He was accompanied by a tall, dark-haired, dark-eyed sophisticate who, while well beyond the blush of youth, could still lay claim to beauty.

"Aunt Margery!" Lady Barbara exclaimed joyfully as the box curtain opened. "I'd no notion you were back in England." She jumped to her feet and flung herself into the other woman's arms.

While this reunion was taking place, Mary Anne stole a furtive glance at Sydney. Her face had paled, but otherwise she managed to appear as though nothing were amiss. Sir Maxwell did not quite match his spouse's poise. The "stone face," in Mary Anne's opinion, looked almost flustered.

Neither did Lord Linley manage to hide his enjoyment of the situation as he made the introductions. "Sydney, m'dear, I don't believe you've yet met Mrs. Edleston. Margery, Lady Cunliffe." The two beauties gave each other the briefest of nods. "And may I present her ladyship's sister, Miss Hawtry? Sir Maxwell is no stranger to you, of course, nor is Captain Rodes. And this gentleman is Lord Littlecote, Miss Hawtry's off-and-on fiancé." His glance slid over the Prussian gentlemen and he shrugged dismissively.

While Littlecote glared daggers, Lord Linley lounged back against a chair back, surveying with a half smile the mischief he had caused. Lady Barbara stepped into the breach to present the Prussians to her aunt.

After these civilities were concluded, Mrs. Edleston turned once more to Lady Cunliffe. "I do beg your ladyship to pardon this intrusion. You see, I had happened to spy my niece across the way and simply could not wait to see her."

Sydney was more than a match for the older woman's smooth sophistication. "Oh, I quite understand." She smiled just as falsely. "And I'm sure you'd like some time alone with Lady Barbara to catch up on family matters. Max, shall we stroll the halls a bit? I admit to being fatigued with sitting already, and the performances have scarce begun." She smiled once more at Mrs. Edleston, whose answering nod acknowledged she'd been outmaneuvered.

"Why, what a capital idea!" Mary Anne saw her opportunity and pounced upon it. "Will you not join me for some exercise, Lord Linley? I've been longing to ask your opinion of a modiste who's been highly recommended. I'm sure you can tell me if she's really all the crack."

"No need to mangle my coat sleeve," Lord Linley protested as she tugged him in the opposite direction from the route her sister and brother-in-law had taken. "Am I supposed to be flattered by your urgency to get me alone? I must confess I find your tactics rather suspect. Still, though, your Lord Littlecote looked sufficiently jealous almost to convince me I possess some fatal charm I've been unaware of."

"I really wish you wouldn't waste our time by talking rubbish. I've something important to speak to you about."

"You do believe in plain dealing, don't you, Miss Hawtry?" He pulled an exquisitely enameled box from the recesses of his coat, put a pinch of snuff upon his wrist, and gracefully inhaled it. "A much more civilized means of enjoying tobacco than blowing a cloud, don't you agree?"

"Oh, bother your tobacco. I wish to speak about my sister's portrait."

He sighed. "I feared you might. Now if I may also speak frankly, my dear Miss Hawtry, I am growing a trifle weary of that subject. Sydney, usually the most delightful of companions, has prosed on and on about the thing to the point of tedium. She—"

"How much do you want for it?" Mary Anne cut in rudely.

"It is not for sale."

"Everything has its price, they say."

" 'They,' then, could never have known the joys of collecting."

74

"Really, Lord Linley? I had not known you were a patron of the arts."

"But then you know very little about me, do you, Miss Hawtry?" As they strolled the crowded corridor, he occasionally returned a bow while more often snubbing any passing acquaintance.

"That's true. Nor do I know very much about art either. Still I doubt that Sydney's portrait is a masterpiece worth keeping."

"Ah, but then, you haven't seen it, have you? I assure you, it's the prize of my collection. And while the term 'masterpiece' may be an overstatement, I am convinced the painting is a true work of art. Why, the flesh tones alone are enough to assure it's merit. For one thing . . ."—he looked down at her slyly—"there's so much of them."

"We will double the amount Sydney lost to you."

"For a dowerless female, you make an extravagant offer, Miss Hawtry. And who, may I ask, is to come up with all that money? Lord Littlecote? Or perhaps the gallant Captain Rodes, who has, I'm given to understand, just lately become wealthy. Sydney herself? Surely not. No doubt my cousin is most generous in the allowance he gives her, but it would hardly cover the price of a great art work. Still, all this speculation is purely academic. The portrait's not for sale."

"Just what then do you intend doing with it?"

"What an odd question to ask, Miss Hawtry. What does one do with a work of art but enjoy it?"

"One shows it off."

He chuckled softly as they slowly reversed their stroll and headed back toward the Cunliffe box. "So that's what's troubling you. Let me set your mind at ease, then. Though the portrait is legally mine, I treat it the same way unscrupulous collectors treat their stolen Rembrandts and their Rubenses. I keep it for my sole enjoyment and only bring it out when I'm quite alone and can worship undisturbed. There's something quite exhilarating, Miss Hawtry, in owning a thing of beauty no one else can see."

"So you don't intend to display it."

"Lady Cunliffe in the nude? You must take me for a blackguard."

He laughed again as Mary Anne's denial stuck in her throat.

"Much as I've enjoyed our chat, Miss Hawtry, don't you think we should conclude it? I see that Maxwell and Sydney are going back inside. It might be a kindness to remove Mrs. Edleston. It pains me to add to the dilemma of so many gossip-mongers. I vow they'll not know which way to look—at Her Royal Highness preening herself—or at Prinny's nose, so noticeably out of joint . . . or at the reunion taking place within your box. I refer of course to the long-delayed meeting between Maxwell's very good friend Mrs. Edleston and . . ."—he paused dramatically—"her charming niece." Once more he indulged in his wicked chuckle. Mary Anne quite longed to kick him.

But the overture had finished before Lord Linley and Mrs. Edleston at last left the Cunliffe box and the party settled back to watch the program. *The Grand Alliance* was followed by *Richard Coeur de Lion*, also chosen to enhance the wave of national pride sweeping over the country.

Mary Anne would have bet a monkey, though, that no one in their party, with the possible exception of the enigmatic Prussians, had a mind fixed upon the stage. It was her opinion that the General and Lady Cunliffe only appeared to be engrossed. They sat side by side like statues, their eyes following the performance, but possibly seeing nothing. She knew Anthony well enough to realize that Mrs. Edleston's appearance had upset him. And Lady Barbara seemed aware of his unease even if she knew nothing of its cause. As for

Lord Littlecote, well, it was obvious that that gentleman was in some sort of a taking.

As if on cue, he now addressed her in what he possibly intended to be an undertone. "Is that the cove?" he growled.

"I beg your pardon?" she whispered back.

"I asked if that's the cove you're supposed to be in love with. I'll tell you right now, Mary Anne, I won't have it. My God, the fellow's nothing but a jackanapes!"

"Lord Linley? Oh, don't be such a pea-goose, Roderick!"

Behind them she heard Anthony's muffled laugh.

# Chapter Nine

"**S**o there you are." *Captain Anthony Rodes carefully shut* the library door behind him as Miss Mary Anne Hawtry, who was curled up in a wing chair by the window, looked up from the book she was reading. "I've been looking everywhere for you."

"Well, that's certainly a switch. I had thought your mission in life was to avoid me."

"That's when my more prudent nature is in control. Now, in spite of my better judgment, I have to talk to you." He pulled up a chair and sat facing her.

"Why do I get the feeling you're about to ring a peal over me?"

"A guilty conscience perhaps?"

"Oh, surely now you aren't annoyed because I arranged for Lord Littlecote to take Lady Barbara to see the Elgin Marbles? She really shouldn't miss them, you know. And since you and Sir Maxwell were supposed to be in Prinny's entourage to Oxford today—by the by, what *are* you doing here?"

"The general gave me leave to attend to some personal business."

"Well, I'd no way of knowing that when I arranged the outing, had I? And I'd meant to go along myself, you know, but I have this frightful headache."

"Yes, I can see you're quite pulled down." He surveyed her blooming health.

"Oh, I took laudanum," she fibbed airily, "and am much, much better. But surely you can't mind that your fiancée has gone sight-seeing with Littlecote. I can assure you it is not at all improper. No one should refine upon it in the least."

"I am well aware, Mary Anne, that you are throwing your fiancé—or whatever he is—at my fiancée's head. But I can tell you right now, it won't wash. Barbara is not about to fall in love with Littlecote."

"You're certainly sure of yourself, sir."

"Not in the least. I just respect Lady Barbara enough to be assured she would not be attracted to that slow-top."

"Roderick is not a slow-top!"

"Oh, no? Well, never mind. That is not what I wished— no, by gad, not *wished* but felt *compelled* to talk to you about. Out with it, Mary Anne. Just what the devil are you up to?"

"I haven't the slightest notion what you're referring to."

"That I doubt. But since you force me to speak plainly, I'm referring to your sudden obsession with thievery. Not only have you probed Littlecote and me on the subject, now it seems you're going around quizzing the servants."

"I'm not quizzing the servants. I just happened to mention the subject to one or two, that's all. But how do you come to know it?"

"O'Toole. That's the trouble with old family retainers, Mary Anne. They do tend to view the people who employ them as rather more than just a source of their bread and butter. He's known you long enough and well enough to suspect you're up to something, and he came to me about it."

"Well, that was certainly presumptuous of him. Whatever I do or don't do has nothing to say to you."

"So I longed to tell him."

"Why didn't you?"

"Because he assumed since I'm the one who played cat's-paw for your chestnuts in the past, I'd be willing to do so now. And, well, I hadn't the heart to disillusion the old fellow. 'If anybody can straighten her out, you can' was what he said."

"How absurd."

"Don't I know it. But here I am, God help me, all the same. So spit it out, Mary Anne. Why are you going around trying to employ a thief?"

"Employ a thief?" Her laughter was glaringly artificial. "Is that what O'Toole told you? Well, that just goes to show how innocent conversations get blown out of all proportion. You heard Lord Littlecote warn us of the crime in London. I just got nervous about it, that's all. And felt the servants should be alerted. I don't see why that should put O'Toole in a taking."

"You were inquiring as to the direction of known housebreakers. Why, Mary Anne?"

"I don't know. What does it matter? Oh, very well, then, curiosity I collect. Littlecote referred to Drury Lane and Tothill Fields as 'thieves' kitchens,' and I just wondered if he knew what he was speaking of, that's all."

She squirmed a bit under the captain's steely stare. She'd

never noticed before that he looked very much like his reverend father.

"Are you or are you not going to tell me what maggot's lodged in your brain?"

"There's nothing to tell," she blustered.

"Very well, then." He rose to his feet. "I've tried. And as you've just pointed out, it's none of my affair. But what I will do, to get you off O'Toole's conscience, is inform the general that you've set Servants' Hall abuzz. And I'll give him my opinion that you're up to no good now. As head of a household that claims you as a close relative, it's his responsibility."

"You wouldn't!"

"Oh, wouldn't I? I can't tell you what pleasure it gives me to wash my hands of the whole affair."

"You can't speak to the general. You mustn't. Oh, please, Anthony. I'm begging you."

Her distress seemed to be far more effective than all her previous denials. He actually looked concerned as he sighed and sat back down. "I think you'd better tell me."

"Oh, very well, then. But first promise me you won't go to Sir Maxwell."

"I'm not going to make any sort of promise till I learn what this is all about. But you must know, God help me, that I'll not do anything purposefully to hurt you. But if it turns out to be a case of the lesser evil—"

"Well, really, Anthony, spare me your sermons. These days I find it hard to understand just why you resisted all your father's efforts to steer you into the Church. You do seem remarkably well suited to the life."

He grinned reluctantly. "Papa will be pleased you think so, but actually I fear I was never meant to be a clergyman. Still, I'm ready to hear your confession nonetheless. So out with it."

Slowly, painfully, and with a great deal of prodding from the captain, Mary Anne poured out the story of the painting. "So it only seems sensible to hire a professional cracksman to get the thing back, don't you see. It's not as if it's really stealing. Lord Linley got the thing under false pretenses after all."

He hardly seemed convinced. "What I really see is that Sydney got herself into this mess, and it's up to her, not you, to get out of it."

"You don't approve of Sydney," she accused. "You never did."

"Whether I approve or disapprove has nothing to say in the matter. But I'll tell you this much—there were plenty of others who thought little of the life she was leading while her husband was away. The general's wife was quite the topic of conversation behind his back, I can assure you. It was well-known she was raising eyebrows over here because of the rackety company she was keeping. It was Lord Linley's name that was most often mentioned."

"Oh, is that so? And tell me, did these same gossip-mongers ever discuss Sir Maxwell and Mrs. Edleston? Oh, but I forgot," she sneered. "Pray do forgive my tactlessness. That particular pattern card of virtue is soon to be your aunt."

"I couldn't say about any of that," he answered stiffly. "But even if it's true that Sir Maxwell seeks his comfort elsewhere, you can hardly blame him, can you?"

"Oh, can I not! And can you possibly explain why you're so open-minded upon that score and so censorious of what you only imagine Sydney has done? It's merely because he's a man, I collect, that you wink at his immorality."

"No!" They were glaring at each other. "If I disapprove of Sydney, it's for a damned good reason. She's broken all the rules. She set out to capture a rich, influential husband and succeeded. Beyond even a Hawtry's wildest dreams, I'd say.'' His gesture took in the gilded plasterwork, the collection of valuable paintings on the walls, the Adam fireplace, the brocade and gilt furniture, the expensive objets d'art all around. ''Besides all this, there's the estate in Hampshire that boasts one of the finest country houses in the whole of England. And to support it all a fortune they say is not just handsome but staggering. So it hardly seems too much to ask that Lady Cunliffe not drag the general's name through the mud.''

''But she didn't! Haven't you been listening to a thing I've said? It wasn't until Sir Maxwell's mistress joined him on the Continent that Sydney began to take the town by storm. And what was she expected to do, sit home and wear the willow? She's young and she's beautiful, so of course she had admirers. But if you believe for a moment she's had lovers, well, you've got maggots in the brain.''

''I've never numbered disloyalty among your faults, Mary Anne.''

''Thank you very much. That brings them down to a million minus one.''

''Am I that hard on you? Well, don't take it to heart. A spurned lover's bound to be a bitter man.

''But let's not stray from the main point here, which happens to be your sister's indiscretions. And at the risk of sounding like my father once again, even you will be hard put to clothe a nude portrait in any sort of respectability.''

''It wasn't precisely nude.''

''Well, close enough, or there wouldn't be all this uproar over it.''

''And only Maxwell was supposed to see it.''

''The artist worked blindfolded no doubt.'' He made the remark sotto voce toward the ceiling.

''A true artist would only view her as a subject.''

''Oh, I see. Merely another bowl of fruit, eh.''

"You think that just because *you* lusted after her—"

"Oh, lord," he groaned. "You aren't going to let me forget that, are you?"

"Why should I care about your carnal desires? You're Lady Barbara's problem."

"That's right, I am. Thank you for the reminder. For I really shouldn't expose myself to the Hawtry contagion much longer. I wouldn't want to come down with another case so soon after recovery."

"Oh, I'm sure you're immune by now." Mary Anne couldn't quite keep the regret out of her voice.

"By all means let's hope so. But back to Lord Linley's painting—"

"It *isn't* Lord Linley's painting. Unstop your ears, won't you. Sydney did not—did *not*, you hear me—have it done for him. And he tricked her into wagering it."

"If you say so." He shrugged.

"There, see. You don't believe me. Men never believe the truth when they hear it." She was looking at him with disgust. "It's all that male conceit, I collect, that makes them cling to their preconceived notions in spite of everything. And if even you insist upon thinking the worst, well, there's no hope from Sir Maxwell. After all the Banbury tales he's been hearing—and I'll bet you anything they were started by Mrs. Edleston—he's bound to jump to the same odious conclusion. So now do you see why I have to get the painting back?"

"No, I don't." He glanced at the clock and stood up.

"You don't have to bolt. Lady Barbara won't catch you out. She's not due home for at least another hour."

"I'm not at all concerned with being 'caught out,' " he replied haughtily. "I can assure you Barbara's mind does not work that way. But I do think this interview has gone on long enough. So I'll just speak my piece and leave."

She stood, too. "All right, then. Let's have the lecture."

"Leave it alone, Mary Anne. If there's any action to be taken, well, it's Sydney's problem, not yours. So for once let her do her own dirty work.

"Besides, I think you're creating a tempest in a teapot. Why don't you simply accept what Lord Linley told you—that he wants the painting for his own, ah, enjoyment and that no one else will ever know of its existence."

"Why don't I simply accept that?" She mimicked his top-lofty tone. "Because Lord Linley Mortlock is not to be trusted as far as I could throw him, that's why. Which, if you were any judge at all of character you'd realize. *I* certainly knew he was a wrong 'un the first time I clapped eyes upon him. And Sydney, who has learned the hard way, says he loves to make mischief for mischief's sake—like bringing your precious Mrs. Edleston to our box and presenting her just to get Sydney's reaction."

"She's not my precious Mrs. Edleston."

"She's your relative-to-be. But never mind that just now. For this thing goes deeper than mere mischief making. I'm telling you that Lord Linley hates Sir Maxwell. And longs to score over him. And what better way to do it than to convince his cousin that Sydney has been his mistress? Oh, he'll make sure the general sees the picture. You can count on that. That's why it has to be stolen. There's no other way."

"No!" he almost thundered. "Stay out of this, Mary Anne. I'm warning you."

"Very well, then. Consider me warned. Go tell O'Toole you've done your prosy duty. And you're right about one thing, Anthony. You have changed. Past recognition. There was a time when you would have helped me steal the thing."

"Well, thank God if I've matured a bit. And it's time you did, too. Besides, I still believe you're making mountains out of molehills."

" 'Tempests in teapots' was your phrase. Let's not mix up the metaphors."

"Whatever. Oh, I grant you Lord Linley's no doubt a scoundrel. But he'd hardly risk the possibility of pistols at dawn."

"Sydney says Maxwell would never call him out. Too much family pride. What he will do is wash his hands of my sister. And she loves him. Oh, I know you don't believe that. But it happens to be true. And right now her happiness—and Savannah's—are the most important things in the world to me."

"Yes, I can see that," he sighed. "And if there was ever a person to go out on a limb for her family, it's you. But please back off for once. The idea of hiring a thief in the same way you'd engage a footman—well, the notion would be comical if it weren't criminal. Forget it, Mary Anne. I want your word you'll do so. I say, are you even listening?"

He moved quite close then in order to take her by the shoulders and give her a little shake. "Pray pay attention. I'm deadly serious, girl. The idea's preposterous. Promise me you'll get that particular maggot out of your head."

She was gazing up into his troubled face, frowning speculatively.

"Mary Anne!"

"Oh, what?" She seemed to snap back to attention.

"You haven't heard a word I've said, have you?"

"Of course I have. Well sort of. I'm sorry, Anthony. I was rather thinking of something else."

He sighed. "Please listen now. I want you to give me your word you'll drop the notion of stealing that cursed painting. Promise me, Mary Anne."

For an answer she rose on tiptoe and carefully placed her lips lightly upon his.

For one brief instant he jerked away. Then his mouth met

hers roughly in an angry kiss that, the longer its duration, threatened to redirect its ferocity into something else. He seemed to sense the danger and at last managed to push her roughly away.

"Damn you, Mary Anne!"

"I am sorry, Anthony. I truly am. I didn't mean to bring on all of this."

"The hell you didn't."

"No, it's true. I swear it. I only wondered what it would be like to kiss you with a mustache. I'd no notion at all you'd react so—strongly. Oddly enough the mustache scarcely seemed to get in the way at all. I'd been thinking that—"

"Go to the devil, Mary Anne," he broke in viciously and with a last furious glare turned on his heel and left her.

Mary Anne collapsed back down upon her chair as her knees suddenly betrayed her. "I probably shall do," she sighed to herself. "There doesn't seem much help for it."

# Chapter Ten

*T*he yellow and black hackney crept slowly down Wych Street, then pulled to a stop before a wooden building tottering on the verge of collapse. The jarvey climbed down from his perch and opened the passenger door. "This is it, miss."

"Are you quite sure?" Mary Anne peered with mounting apprehension at the filthy, cracked windowpanes that afforded only a blurred view of the patrons inside the coffeehouse. Such a muting, she'd begun to suspect as they'd woven their way through the disreputable neighborhood off Drury Lane, was most likely merciful. An assignation in a place devoted to a nonintoxicating beverage had once sounded perfectly respectable. Now she was having third and fourth thoughts.

The jarvey read her mind. "Like I was saying, miss, you've

got no business in this part of town. Best let me take you 'ome.''

"Could you come in with me?" She looked at the burly coachman hopefully.

"Lor', not on your life, miss. Why, they'd strip me coach in no time if I was to turn me back on it. They'd likely 'ave the shoes right off me 'orses. No, call me a liar. The truth is that's the last I'd see of me cattle *or* their shoes, and that's a fact. No, I'll take you 'ome, that's wot I'll do, and I wouldn't say fairer to me own daughter.''

"No, thank you." Mary Anne was climbing out of the hackney, placing her feet carefully among the unspeakable refuse of the street. "It's most vital that I talk to someone in there. Has to do with one of the servants, you see.''

Well, that wasn't *exactly* a whisker, she salved her conscience, which had taken on the guise of the Reverend Mr. Rodes. One of the servants *was* involved. It was the thirteen-year-old kitchen maid who'd hissed at her from the back stairway and confided that her sister's husband had been sent to Newgate for a robbery planned by a certain Mr. Wakley. Ned Wakley, according to little Katy, was a nonesuch in his line of work. When Mary Anne had pointed out that he couldn't be quite up to snuff if her relative was now in prison for the caper he'd planned, the servant had replied "Yes, but they didn't nab Ned Wakley, now, did they, miss?" Which was, Mary Anne supposed, a recommendation of a kind.

The pandemonium inside the coffeehouse hushed immediately as she crossed the threshold. A squalling fishwife of a woman paused in the act of climbing over a tall wooden bench back in order to scratch the eyes out of a cursing rival on the other side. The gallows birds crowded expectantly around the would-be combatants redirected their attention to the intruder. A slovenly fat woman whose mammoth breasts were blousing over her filthy bodice allowed her muffin to scorch on her toasting fork as she gaped at Mary Anne. Indeed the only occupants of the room who seemed to be oblivious of her presence were a couple making love on one of the back benches. Miss Hawtry turned red and averted her eyes while muttered terms like 'Covent Garden nun' and "gentry-mort," along with others she did not care to contemplate the meaning of, struck her ears.

A tall, stooped man with rolled-up sleeves and a dirty apron was filling a mug from the spigot of an enormous vat set over those coals the muffin woman was using. He must be the proprietor, Mary Anne concluded. She screwed up her courage and approached him. "If you please, sir, I'm trying to locate a Mr. Ned Wakley." She had hoped to speak confidentially, but in the sudden stillness her voice seemed to reverberate throughout the room. "I was told I might find him here."

"And who told you a thing like that, miss?"

"You might say it was a business acquaintance of Mr. Wakley. It's most important that I locate him. Can you help me?"

"Well, now, miss, I'd say that all depends." His eyes focused significantly upon her reticule.

She was mentally calculating just how much she could possibly spare from it while at the same time wondering if he and the others would not most likely help themselves to its entire contents anyway when a voice interrupted.

"Never ye mind, Jack, old friend. If it's all the same to ye, I'll identify myself."

Mary Anne turned toward the voice to see a tiny ferret of a man with a pinched nose and chin, small black eyes, and scraggly muttonchops extract himself from a table. His top hat was battered, its brim uncurled. His coat was two sizes too large for him and threadbare. She looked him over with a sinking sensation. She had expected something on more heroic lines. A Dick Turpin type, for instance.

"You wanted a word, miss?"

The man was no taller than herself Mary Anne saw as he walked toward her. They could have looked each other straight in the eye if this sort of directness had been in the little man's nature. Instead, his black, sharp glims darted here and there, but never came to rest anywhere near her range.

"I have a business proposition to discuss and a hackney coach waiting outside. Perhaps we'd best ride around a bit while I tell you of it."

The jarvey didn't try to hide his disapproval as he opened the coach door and handed Mary Anne inside. The scowl he focused upon Mr. Wakley sent the black eyes skittering from sky to curb and back behind him to the coffeehouse, then down the street to where a bucket of slops was being emptied from an upstairs window. But even so, he seemed to realize he'd been given a warning. He oozed gingerly into the coach and sat as far from Mary Anne as possible.

She came directly to the point. "I need you to recover some property for me that's in somebody else's house."

"Burglary? I don't go in for that sort of thing no more, miss. I'm wot ye might call reformed. Thinking of joining the chapel I am." Mr. Wakley's attempt to look virtuous met with dubious success. But his ubiquitous gaze did at last come to light, focused upon her reticule.

She sighed inwardly. It was obvious her meager resources weren't going to be adequate. She'd hoped to keep Sydney in the dark about her scheme, but it now appeared likely she'd have to apply to her sister to finance the theft.

"I can assure you," she bargained, "there's nothing about this business to bother your conscience over. The gentleman who now has my property got it under false pretenses."

"That ain't likely to make the Charlies treat me any better if they nab me, miss."

"Well, I was told you were very good at your trade, Mr. Wakley. I was trusting you'd not get caught."

This appeal to his professional pride seemed to have some small effect. "And just wot's the nature of this property, miss?"

Mary Anne described the painting, and he whistled at its size. But the real consternation came when he learned it was located in St. James's Square.

"Robbing a swell in a place like that! Botany Bay won't even come into the picture. That's a 'anging offense, that is."

This aspect of the enterprise she hadn't dwelled on. "I didn't suppose you'd get caught," she repeated. "I was led to believe you did this sort of thing routinely."

"I don't go around nimming valuable art from gentry coves." He sniffed virtuously.

"Very well, then." She caved in suddenly, having no heart to put anyone into jeopardy. "I'll tell the driver to take us back. Just forget I ever mentioned it."

" 'Old on a bit. Let's not get too 'asty, miss," Mr. Wakley protested as she was leaning toward the window to shout at the jarvey. "I wasn't saying as I wouldn't do it. I was merely pointing out the perils of wot you 'ave in mind, so as you could see that the price I 'ave in mind is only reasonable. A job like that, I'd say, would be worth at least five hundred pounds."

"Five hundred pounds!"

" 'Azard pay, miss."

"Well, it certainly won't be that hazardous. In fact, the way I've worked it out there should be very little risk at all. You'll remove the painting the night of the first, you see, during all the celebrations. Nobody will want to miss the

92

mock battle they'll be having on the serpentine. Lord Linley Mortlock's bound to give his servants permission to attend. Why, you should be able to waltz right in and take the painting, safe as houses. Two hundred pounds should easily cover that much hazard.''

"Hmmmm." The ferret eyes danced here and there while Mr. Wakley thought the matter over. "Four hundred pounds!" was his conclusion.

"Three hundred."

"Done!"

Mary Anne poked her head out the window and directed the driver to take them back to Wych Street. After a bit more haggling, clinched by the fact that fifty pounds was all her reticule contained, Mr. Wakley agreed he would take this on account and receive the rest once he'd delivered the painting into her hands. They parted amicably enough in front of the coffeehouse.

The coachman sprang his horses, wanting to see the last of that neighborhood, and Mary Anne finally allowed herself the luxury she'd longed for from her first moment of contact with Mr. Wakley. She held her perfumed handkerchief to her nose.

She instructed the driver to let her out at Hyde Park Corner in order not to have to explain to anyone just why she'd gone abroad in a hackney coach. But as it happened, the precaution proved unnecessary. There was no one going in or out to see her.

Indeed she'd begun to think the entire household was absent till she heard a murmur of voices coming from the library. One, she believed, was Sydney's. And the sooner she let her sister know she would be needing three hundred pounds, the sooner Sydney could go about raising it. She only hoped the other would agree it was a small enough price to pay to save her marriage.

But as she approached the doorway, which was slightly ajar, she recognized the voices as Littlecote's and Lady Barbara's. She peeped through the crack between the hinges and was able to see the pair, seated side by side on the settee in earnest conversation. She congratulated herself that at least one of her schemes was working. Certainly the two of them looked quite comfortable together. Lady Barbara was tambouring while she listened to his lordship with rapt attention. Mary Anne was just about to tiptoe away lest she interrupt such a happy state of affairs when she heard her own name mentioned. She paused, shamelessly, to listen.

"I must confess I was at a loss to know just what your relationship was to this household, Lord Littlecote," Lady Barbara was saying. "But Captain Rodes informs me that you are Miss Hawtry's fiancé. Oh, dear, have I perhaps spoken out of turn?"

Mary Anne did not wish to risk another peek, so she could only conclude that Roderick's expression must have changed.

"I assumed the betrothal had been announced," her ladyship continued, "but now I realize the captain didn't say so."

"Oh, the notice was in the *Gazette* all right." Lord Littlecote's voice was angry.

"I see."

"Don't expect you do, actually. The thing is, Mary Anne—Miss Hawtry—wants to cry off."

"Oh, dear. I'm dreadfully sorry. Please believe me, Lord Littlecote, I had not meant to pry." Lady Barbara sounded quite distressed.

"I know you didn't. That's quite all right." His voice was gruff with emotion. "As a matter of fact, I'm glad you brought the matter up. Been longing to talk to someone about it."

"But really, Lord Littlecote, I don't think I'm the proper person."

"Why ever not? I realize we ain't long acquainted, but I know you well enough to see what a sympathetic sort you are. Why, look at the way you've put up with those Prussian coves. Enough to drive anybody else right into a strait-jacket—all those guten tags and danke schöns." He shuddered. "But you don't let it bother you in the least. So you see, Lady Barbara, you're exactly the kind of person a cove can talk to."

"Very well, then, if you feel it would help."

Mary Anne concluded that her ladyship was most uncomfortable.

"The thing is," Littlecote blurted out, "she says she can't marry me because she's in love with somebody else."

"Oh, how dreadful for you!"

"Yes, it is actually. Damned embarrassing, don't you know, what with everyone knowing about the betrothal. Makes a man feel all sorts of a bloody fool. Oh, sorry! Shouldn't have used that word. Don't know what came over me. Beg pardon, your ladyship."

"That's quite all right, Lord Littlecote. I quite understand how upset you must be feeling. But really there's no reason for you to feel any sort of a fool. The matter does not reflect upon you in the least if Miss Hawtry loves another." She paused delicately. "Of course if your heart is engaged, well, that's a different matter."

"Oh, it ain't so much a matter of being brokenhearted." (Here Mary Anne glared in the direction of the voice.) "Though I'll admit she pretty well bowled me off my feet when I first clapped eyes on her at her come-out."

"Miss Hawtry is quite beautiful," Lady Barbara murmured. "She and her sister are both dazzling, in fact. They cast every other female in the shade."

"Not in your case," he responded gallantly.

Her laugh was embarrassed. "Oh, dear. I just now realized how that must have sounded. Pray believe I was not actually fishing for compliments. Now, then. You were telling me about Miss Hawtry's come-out."

"Not much to tell. I was shopping the marriage mart, and I'd never seen such a stunning female. And I don't mind saying it was flattering to be able to cut the other fellows out."

"I can well imagine."

"Of course I knew all along that she was dangling after a rich husband. Has to, you know. Not a feather in the family to fly with. Though, when it comes down to it," he added practically, "I expect Sir Maxwell will at least settle a competency on her. Not that I count on it, you understand. No, I decided then and there that Miss Hawtry was the one for me. And I wouldn't listen to a word when I was warned against her. And after all that I can tell you I don't much appreciate being made to look the fool."

Mary Anne could well imagine his platter-faced expression.

"I still think you take a wrong view of the matter, Lord Littlecote." The other's murmur was quite soothing. "I'm sure Miss Hawtry cannot help it if she loves someone else. Love is blind, they say. Her attachment in no way reflects upon you."

"Oh, you think not?" Littlecote's voice was vicious. "Just wait till you hear who she's fallen in love with."

The hallway suddenly lurched, and Mary Anne grabbed the door frame for support. She almost gasped aloud.

"Oh, but Lord Littlecote, I don't think I *should* hear."

"Yes, you should. Need to understand just why the matter's put me into such a taking. The little simpleton thinks she's in love with Lord Linley Mortlock, that's who."

This time Mary Anne had to clap both hands over her mouth.

"Lord Linley? But surely not."

"Defies all reason, don't it? The man's a regular rakehell. Why, he and her own sister—but the least said about that the better. Anyhow, to be tossed aside for a scoundrel like that—well, I'll tell you, Lady Barbara, it's the outside of enough and I'll not have it." His voice had risen.

"Yes, I can see where it would be most upsetting. For I must own I do not find Lord Linley in the least appealing. And I'm amazed Miss Hawtry, who seems a very sensible sort, would do so. But if he is indeed her choice, would it not be best in the long run for you simply to accept it?"

"No, by gad! What I intend to do is wait around till the little gudgeon comes to her senses. I ain't about to—"

Just then Mary Anne heard the sound of approaching voices and silently backtracked to the entryway. When Sir Maxwell came down the steps with his daughter clinging to his hand, he might have supposed his sister-in-law was entering from the street.

"We're just about to join the parade on Rotten Row. At least I assume people still ride out in London during the fashionable hour."

"Oh, yes. It's still all the crack to be seen in the park at five."

"Won't you join us?" he asked courteously.

"Oh, is Sydney coming, too?"

The moment the question blurted past her lips Mary Anne felt ready to sink.

Her brother-in-law might suddenly have put on a mask. "No, your sister is otherwise engaged." His voice was as unrevealing as his face. "But we'd be delighted to have the other beautiful Miss Hawtry along."

Mary Anne's excuse, that she planned to write a letter to

97

their mother in Ireland, was a lame one. But since the invitation was a mere formality, it sufficed. She kissed her tiny niece good-bye and stood watching while a footman sprang to open the door for the soldier and his child. She then proceeded thoughtfully up the stairs.

Poor Sydney, to be in love with a man who could not tolerate the mere mention of her name. And if the husband and wife were estranged at this point, what would their lives be like if he should learn of the scandalous portrait? The effect of such a discovery upon their fragile marriage didn't bear thinking on.

Still, there was one bright spot, she thought as she walked into her bedchamber and untied the ribbons of her poke bonnet. If one could only look at it that way. At least Sydney was bound to agree that three hundred pounds was, after all, a small price to pay to keep such an eventuality from ever happening.

# Chapter
# Eleven

*The rumor was that His Royal Highness had become more* than a little wearied of the peace celebration. If so, the blame for this attitude could be laid squarely at the door of the foreign nobility.

Things had gone badly from the very first. The Grand Duchess Catherine had traveled to England ahead of the Czar, and she and the Regent had taken an immediate and intense dislike to each other. Nor had she endeared herself to the English people with her imperious rudeness. The Czar's 'platter-faced sister' Lord Clancarty had called her. Then to make matters worse, when Alexander himself had arrived, he'd refused to stay at St. James's Palace, as arranged, but had insisted upon joining his sister at Pulteney's instead. Even King Frederick of Prussia, a bluff, soldierly type, did not fall in completely with the Prince's arrangements. While he did stay at Clarence House, he failed to make use of the suite of satinwood furniture installed especially for him and asked for a spartan camp bed instead. For once the Regent and his subjects were in complete accord. They were all finding the foreign visitors a royal pain.

But now the English had their own reason to celebrate. After a five year absence, Lord Wellington had come home, and the country had gone wild.

When the duke's ship had entered Dover Harbor, every square foot of the shore was occupied by an excited, cheering crowd. And the sixty miles of dusty turnpike that led to London was flanked by a solid double line of Wellington's enthusiastic fellow subjects. His progression from coast to capital was one long roaring cheer.

No one in London was more aware of the hero's return than the folk at Cunliffe House. They had found it difficult to come and go because of the crowds collected around Apsley House next door in hopes that Wellington might be spied there visiting his elder brother. And they had been invited to the Carlton House fete the Regent was giving to honor the conquering hero. Say what one would of Prinny, a gala at his own residence could be expected to outdo all the other entertainments that had heretofore taken place.

In view of the crush of traffic anticipated for the affair, Sir Maxwell had suggested that his entire party try and squeeze into one carriage, that was, if the ladies were not too afraid of mussing their gowns.

"Perhaps I should sit on your knee, Max," Sydney suggested rather maliciously, as Lady Barbara, Mary Anne, Lord Littlecote, and the two Prussians packed themselves inside.

"An excellent suggestion, m'dear," her husband replied evenly.

Squeezed as she was between Littlecote and the older Prussian, Mary Anne watched uneasily. Her sister seemed to be deliberately tantalizing her husband, clinging tightly to him, as though in peril of suddenly sliding off his satin knee breeches. Mary Anne suspected this was the closest the two had been since the night of his return. She did know he still slept in his dressing room. "Don't snag your gown on my medals" was his only comment as his wife snuggled closer.

"Why, where is Anthony—Captain Rodcs, I mean to say?" Mary Anne asked in an attempt to take attention away from whatever drama was being enacted between the husband and the wife. She immediately wished she'd picked a different topic. Or perhaps she only imagined that Lady Barbara had reacted to the familiar usage of her fiancé's first name.

She answered pleasantly enough, though. "He had urgent business that needed his attention."

"I'm to blame, I fear." Sir Maxwell spoke between the ostrich feathers his wife was wearing in her hair. "I sent him to Windsor with a message. I had thought he'd be back by now. I ask your forgiveness, Lady Barbara."

She smiled and nodded. Mary Anne once again noted with a jealous pang how genuinely sweet-natured her ladyship was.

"Just as well, actually." Lord Littlecote tried to shift to a more comfortable position as they inched down the street in the crush of carriages, and was unable to quite manage it. "Never been laced up in a corset, but I expect this is exactly what it feels like."

Everyone laughed except the Prussians, who looked politely puzzled. After Lady Barbara had translated the remark, they echoed the merriment. "Oh, for God's sake," Littlecote sniffed in an audible aside.

Two thousand guests had been invited to the fete, and the Cunliffe party could only applaud Sir Maxwell's good judgment in reducing the traffic jam by one. As it was, they felt it prudent to leave their coach some distance from Carlton

House and proceed on foot in order to arrive at the designated hour of nine.

If the Prussians had hoped to return home and boast of their visit to Carlton House, they were doomed to disappointment. For once past His Royal Highness's portals, the hordes of guests were being ushered around the palace into the garden where a special polygonal building had been erected for the occasion. No common tent would suffice for the extravagant Regent. This was a solid structure built of brick and topped with a leaded roof. But as the guests filed inside, the illusion was that they were not indoors at all but had somehow been transported into a magic fairy garden.

Looking glasses, gracefully draped in muslin, ranged over the walls and reflected back the sparkle of a dozen chandeliers, giving the effect of summer light and airiness. A temple loomed before them, constructed of huge banks of flowers whose fragrance mingled with the smell of melting tallow to create an exotic, heady perfume. Music filled the room as if by magic, emanating through leaf and petal walls that concealed two orchestras. *"Wunderbar!"* the younger Prussian gentleman exclaimed while the other members of their group murmured similar English sentiments.

Staying together as a group while attempting to drink in all the splendor proved impossible. The Cunliffe party was soon separated by the press of other guests pushing their way through, seeking friends or merely elbowing for a better vantage point. At one moment, Lord Littlecote had been at Mary Anne's side; at the next she and Sydney had been abandoned.

They were admiring the floral temple when a familiar voice purred behind them "Ah, ill met by moonlight, proud Titania." They turned to confront the mocking gaze of Lord Linley Mortlock. His lordship was escorting Mrs. Edleston, a vision in a low-cut black crape gown figured with black satin. The wealth of diamonds that adorned her neck, coiffure, and ears rivaled the sparkle of the many mirrors. The ladies gave each other the briefest of nods, the merest tight-lipped smiles.

"Forgive me, Sydney m'dear, for the salutation," his lordship smirked. "You could never be 'ill met,' of course. But you must admit that all this . . ."—his sweeping gesture was underscored by a pained expression—"is simply too *Midsummer Night's Dream*ish for words."

"I think it's lovely."

"Oh, well then. His Highness is to be congratulated on his ability to please where it matters most. And I must say you do look stunning, my dear." His appreciation of her white lace over satin ensemble seemed sincere. "Shakespeare's Titania come to life in her proper element. By the by, I do not spy your Oberon around. How could he ever bear to leave your side?"

"Are you possibly referring to Maxwell, Lord Linley? Don't you think you're overdoing the *Midsummer Night's Dream* motif? If you persist, we might be forced to cast our own Nick Bottom."

"To turn into an ass? Well now, Lord Littlecote does rather spring to mind. But you're right of course, dear Sydney, I am becoming boring with this tiresome little conceit. So if you beautiful ladies will excuse us, Mrs. Edleston and I shall go in search of Lord Wellington. One should have at least a glimpse of the hero of the hour. But if we can't find him in all this mob scene, we'll simply have to make do with Maxwell, our own pet hero, won't we? No doubt we shall see you two again. The refreshment tent perhaps? In the meantime: 'We do wander everywhere, Swifter than the moonës sphere.' Oh, I beg your pardon. There I go again. Can't seem to help myself. Till later, then." He blew a kiss toward the sisters as he steered Mrs. Edleston through the crowd.

Mary Anne and Sydney stood where they were long

enough for the pair to be out of sight. "I can't begin to express just how much I loathe that underbred, overly conceited—" Sydney had begun in a low voice quivering with emotion when she was interrupted by an old acquaintance, and Mary Anne was left to wonder just which of the two, Lord Linley or Mrs. Edleston, she meant.

She thought it best, though, not to raise the question once Sydney's friend had moved along. Instead, she stood on tiptoe, gazing round the room. "The others must have left," she said. "We'd best try and find them."

"Why?"

It was, on contemplation, a fair question. Mary Anne could think of no compelling reason why they should spend the evening in the company of those they came with. Except, perhaps, for one. She voiced it. "But shouldn't you be with Sir Maxwell?"

"Why?"

Sydney might have been some barefoot philosopher the way she kept hurling that question back in her sister's teeth.

"Well, because he's your husband, I suppose."

Lady Cunliffe tossed her beautiful head. "Perhaps you should remind *him* of that. He left me quickly enough, you may have noticed."

Mary Anne nipped off a sigh. The momentary lift of spirits she had felt upon entering the Carlton House gardens had quite vanished, and she was once again blue-deviled. She did wish Anthony had come. No, she did not! Seeing him in tandem with Lady Barbara would really be the outside of enough.

"Oh, don't look so glum, little sister." Sydney gave her arm a playful shake. "I had not meant to spoil your evening. I certainly intend to enjoy myself. This is, after all, a celebration. Rule, Britannia, and all that! Come on. Let's go find the champagne. There's bound to be some somewhere."

They left the polygon by way of a walk decked out in green calico. Its walls were lined with allegorical transparencies. They paused before one called *The Overthrow of Tyranny by the Allied Powers*, then moved along to admire *Military Glory*.

By the time they had absorbed all of these wonders, the sisters' moods had lightened. They joined the flow of guests strolling down a covered promenade decorated with draperies and rose-colored cords. It led them to a Corinthian temple purposefully erected to house a marble bust of the Duke of Wellington. The sculpture was placed upon a column before an enormous-looking glass engraved with a star and the letter *W*.

"I'd give anything to have seen the duke's face when he saw it," Sydney gurgled. "Somehow I doubt he sees himself as a Greek-god type."

They were still smiling about the deification as they left that walk to go in search of other wonders. "Where *is* the refreshment room?" Sydney wondered. "I'm about to perish of thirst."

"Most of the crowd is going in that direction," Mary Anne pointed out practically, and once more they joined a procession of slowly moving guests.

"Goodness, I'm beginning to feel like a school of fish," Sydney complained in her sister's ear after they'd crept on awhile.

"School of snails, you mean," the other replied, wondering how best to get around two corpulent couples who took up the entire walkway.

"There's no such thing. But come on. This should lead us somewhere." Sydney gave her sister's hand a tug toward an unlit gravel path that angled off from the main walkway. "This should be a shortcut."

"No doubt. But where to?"

"Oh, who cares." Sydney struck out briskly. "At least we have it to ourselves. That's sufficient recommendation. I've had enough of crowds to last me for—" She broke off with a gasp and stopped so abruptly that Mary Anne ran smack into her.

The path had led to a small grotto where a marble fountain splashed out a staccato rhythm. The only light in this part of the garden came from the full moon overhead. It was enough. It quite sufficed to illuminate the embracing couple.

Sydney wheeled and gave her sister a push back in the direction they'd come from. But Mary Anne did not turn away quite fast enough to prevent her horrified gaze from locking with Sir Maxwell's. It seemed equally as stricken as her own.

Later that night as she lay awake it was those eyes that haunted her. "Well, he should have been upset," she thought viciously. Betraying Sydney that way. And did he suppose Sydney hadn't known of his infidelity till then? What beasts men were anyhow! After Lady Barbara and Anthony were married, would he also—? She pushed that thought resolutely from her mind and tried for a more comfortable position flat on her stomach with her head underneath her pillow to shut out the moonlight streaming into the room. It didn't help. Her mind kept racing.

What was to become of them? Would Sydney's unhappiness lead her into more and more indiscretions till she actually became the kind of woman the gossip-mongers labeled her? And as for herself . . . well, that didn't bear thinking on at the moment. One thing was clear at least: their mother had a great deal to answer for. Look where her insistence upon brilliant matches had landed both her daughters. No, even that wasn't fair. She and Sydney were responsible for their own lives. They had made their choices. Or she had at any rate. There was no use blaming—

The pillow had prevented her from hearing the chamber door ease open or the soft footsteps approach her bed. But a light touch on her arm sent her leaping upright, and Anthony's hand barely clapped upon her mouth in time to bottle up a shriek. "It's all right. It's me," he whispered.

It was not all right! Sneaking into a lady's bedchamber in the dead of night! Who did he think she was, anyhow, another Mrs. Edleston? She was removing his hand in order to give him a good piece of her mind when the sight of him there in the moonlight stopped her cold. "What on earth?" she blurted.

"Keep your voice down."

He was dressed most oddly in an ill-cut, short dark coat buttoned to the chin. She could have sworn she'd seen O'Toole wearing one just like it. His trousers were also black, as was the stocking cap he wore. Just as she was about to ask if he'd been to a peculiar masquerade of some sort, she saw that the left side of his face was raked with scratches. One especially deep one was oozing blood.

"Oh, dear heavens, you're hurt," she whispered, and before thinking properly, she'd snatched off her white cotton nightcap and was dabbing his face with it.

"That was brilliant," he said dryly. "Just how do you hope to explain your cap's condition?"

"I'll think of something. Right now I'm more concerned about your explanations. What on earth has happened to your face?" She dabbed at the blood once more.

"It came into contact with some thorny shrubbery when I jumped from an upstairs window."

"You did what!"

His hand clamped once more, roughly, over her mouth. "Mary Anne," he said between clenched teeth, "I've had a very long and trying night and unless you want me to smother you with that pillow, please keep your voice down." He was suddenly diverted. "By the by, how in God's name do you manage to breathe, sleeping like that?"

"Never mind that now. If you don't tell me what's happened to you, I swear I *will* scream."

"What's happened to me? Oh, nothing really." He sat down upon the edge of her bed. "I've just been out doing that spot of burglary you wanted done, that's all."

"Oh, Anthony, how famous!" And without giving bedchambers, nightdresses, the time of evening, or sleeping fiancées a thought, Mary Anne spontaneously reached out and hugged him. "You've stolen the painting for me. Oh, how marvelous!"

He untwined her arms. His face was bitter. "No 'Are you all right, Anthony?' No 'Are the Charlies after you, Anthony?' Just 'You've stolen the painting for me, how marvelous.' "

"I asked how you were before. And I ruined my nightcap."

"She ruined her nightcap," he informed the ceiling. "I've damned near killed myself, not to mention barely escaping—for the moment at least—being hauled off to prison. But Miss Hawtry here has ruined her nightcap. My own sacrifices pale by comparison."

"I was merely pointing out, you sap-skull, that I did show my concern. Now will you stop rattling and tell me what you've done with Sydney's portrait?"

"Since I didn't get it," he answered sullenly, "I haven't done anything with it."

"Oh."

The monosyllable expressed an entire volume of disappointment.

"Well, I am sorry, Miss Hawtry, if my expertise as a

second-story man didn't quite rise to your expectations. But I can almost assure you it isn't in Lord Linley's rooms. I'd searched the place pretty thoroughly before he caught me.''

"He caught you!" she gasped.

"That's what I said. Did you think I'd taken up jumping out of first-floor windows from a sudden urge to become a circus performer? I can assure you that desire never—''

"Anthony!" She reached out, grabbed his shoulder, and shook him. "If you don't immediately tell me everything that's happened, I swear I'll *push* you from this first-floor window. And start from the very beginning this time.''

"The beginning? It was when I moved to Stanton Rectory. You were five, as I recall, and started bear-leading me immediately.''

"Anthony!" Her voice rose dangerously.

"Oh, very well. The beginning is that the more I thought about it, the more I agreed with you, God help me, that Sir Maxwell must never know about the painting. And I feared you were probably right that Lord Linley would somehow contrive to let him see it. And I also realized, from scores of bitter experiences, that you weren't likely to let the matter rest. I concluded that you'd try to recover the thing and botch the job. So I felt I owed it to the general to take care of the matter myself.''

"Well, I never supposed you did it for me," Mary Anne lied bitterly. "But your success hardly seems spectacular, I'd say.''

"I didn't get it because it wasn't there," he was stung into retorting. "For a law-abiding citizen, I'd actually worked the thing out rather well. I'd picked a time when I knew his dandified lordship would be at Carlton House. It never occurred to me that a butterfly like that would leave a party early. And I also thought any servants who stayed at home would take advantage of his absence by partying in Servants'

Hall themselves. I was right about that, at least," he added with some satisfaction. "So all I had to do was ease quietly through a ground-floor window. Then I went upstairs and found his lordship's bedchamber."

"His bedchamber? Whatever for?"

"Because that's where any normal man would keep a thing like that."

"That's disgusting."

"If you say so. Anyhow, it wasn't there. So I went to his picture gallery. By the by, he really does have a nice collection. But your sister's—life study—is definitely not among it. He does have a Turner, though, that was my downfall. I'd stopped to admire it and didn't hear his lordship come in. *He's* the one you should hire for your next burglary. The damned fellow moves like a cat. He saw me, let out a screech, and I'd barely time to land him a facer—flattened him, I'm happy to say—and dive for the window when I heard his servants running."

"Oh, my goodness! Did he recognize you?"

"Don't see how he could have. I was wearing a mask. It got ripped off by the cursed thornbush when I landed, but it was still in place when Lord Linley surprised me.

"Anyhow, I unstuck myself from the bushes and hared off down the street with his lordship's footmen in full cry. I had to run in the opposite direction from here, of course, and even after I'd given 'em the slip, I thought it best to stay away from Cunliffe House awhile just in case his lordship got suspicious enough to have them watch this place. So what with one thing and another, it's been a devilish long night."

"Oh, Anthony, I'm so sorry."

"You're only sorry I failed."

"That isn't so and you know it."

"Do I? Well, that part really doesn't matter. The thing is, at least we know your sister's portrait isn't on display in St.

James's Square. So you might as well give Lord Linley the benefit of the doubt and accept what he says as truth. He doesn't plan to flaunt the thing. Anyhow, I now wash my hands of the matter, Mary Anne. Will you please accept that as final?''

''Yes, of course. And even if you don't believe it, I am sorry for all you've been through. I never really meant— I didn't really think— Oh, Anthony, if anything had happened to you, I'd never have forgiven myself.'' This night had been altogether too trying. Tears welled up in her eyes and spilled over.

''Oh, for God's sake, don't cry,'' he said huskily. ''I didn't intend to upset you. Never suspected I could. Crying's really not in your line. At least it never used to be.'' He dabbed ineffectually at her eyes with the bloodied nightcap, then tossed it aside and took her in his arms to kiss the tears away.

What had started out quite tenderly was getting rather out of hand when Mary Anne collected her wits enough to give him a push that sent him reeling off the bed. By dent of admirable agility he somehow managed to land upon his feet.

''You don't have to get so violent. I wasn't about to 'despoil' you, you know.''

''No, I didn't know.'' Mary Anne adjusted her nightdress, the ribbons of which had somehow come undone.

''If that was my intent, I'd have done it years ago.''

''What an odious thing to say!''

''Just trying to point out that my intentions have always been honorable. And if I forget myself here for a moment, I don't wish you to think it will become habit-forming. I'm betrothed, and there's no way I can honorably get out of it. It's too late for us, Mary Anne. So why don't you mend your fences with Littlecote. He's not such a bad sort really. And I do wish you happy. But there's one more thing you should know. In spite of my conduct just now, I intend to take my marriage vows seriously. I won't cheat, Mary Anne."

She glared indignantly in the cold moonlight. "Are you by any chance implying that *I* would?"

He shrugged. "Well, it's in the blood, you know."

Nothing Captain Rodes had faced that entire evening, neither housebreaking nor pursuit, had put him in such peril. Involuntarily he backed off from the fury in Miss Hawtry's eyes. "I was referring to your mother, not Sydney, you know. It's no secret she was Lord Carswell's mistress for years before his wife conveniently died and he married her."

"Get out!" Mary Anne ordered. "You get out of here this instant or by heaven I'll scream rape."

Anthony obviously believed her. Or at any rate he didn't choose to discuss the matter further. Even Napoléon Bonaparte's retreat was no more ignominious than the British captain's swift withdrawal.

# Chapter
# Twelve

"I'm sure he rides out every day just to see her," Lady Cunliffe informed her sister.

"Well, I wish him luck trying to spot anyone in this crush."

Rotten Row was, as usual, teeming during the fashionable hour. Carriages vied with high-stepping bits of blood for the right of way, then blocked traffic as their occupants paused to hail acquaintances among the crowd of *ton*nish strollers that flanked the drive. But few if any of the stylish throng cut quite the dash the Hawtry sisters cut.

Lady Cunliffe was driving her own rig, a sky blue curricle with creamy leather fittings. She was wearing a carriage dress of that same shade of blue, accessorized by a cream-colored Parisian bonnet. "Are you quite certain you want me to come along?" Mary Anne had exclaimed when she first saw her. "Won't I spoil the whole effect?"

Sydney had looked her coolly up and down, appraising her gray bombazine high dress and chip-straw bonnet. "It's all right; you'll match the horses," she had quipped. "Otherwise you'd have to walk, little sister."

As they drove along between rows of stately trees, still dripping from a recent shower, Mary Anne admired the skill it took for Sydney to weave in and out among the traffic. She went white as a sheet, however, when her sister forced her team to a sudden halt to give right-of-way to a small boy in pursuit of a wayward dog.

"It's all right. You can breathe now."

"My word, you are a nonesuch!"

"Nothing to it. I like driving. Want me to teach you?"

"Oh, would you?" Mary Anne's eyes shone. "I'd like it above all things." But the elation was short-lived. "Not that I expect to ever have a rig of my own to drive."

"You could have if you'd be sensible and marry Littlecote."

"That's odd advice for you to give."

"It's the same advice I've been giving all along."

"Yes, but it carried more weight before I learned you yourself had married for love." She gasped and held on for dear life as Sydney headed toward a narrow opening between a phaeton and a gig.

"Never suspected you were so hen-hearted." Sydney grinned once the maneuver had been successfully concluded.

"Well, I may not be deliriously happy at the moment, but let me assure you, I do not long for death."

"Nor do I. How did Shakespeare put it? 'Men have died from time to time and worms have eaten them, but not for love.' That observation can apply to women just as well. Which brings me back to the point I was making. You said just now I married for love. Well, you can see all the good it's done me." Her lip curled. "So be careful you don't lose

114

Littlecote with all your scheming. A fiancé in the hand, remember, is worth two Anthonys in the bush.''

"How on earth did you find out about Anthony in the bush?''

"I'm just updating the old saying about a bird in the hand, you pea-goose.''

"Oh. I thought you'd somehow heard—well, never mind.'' She giggled nervously at the memory of Anthony's literal encounter with the proverb's shrubbery.

"Will you please stop straying from the point. I'm trying to do my sisterly duty and warn you not to let Littlecote slip through your net. It's becoming obvious that you go to all sorts of lengths to avoid him. Where is he right now, by the by?''

"You'll not believe it when I tell you.''

"Try me.''

"He's giving English lessons to the Prussians.''

"You're bamming me!''

"S'truth. He says it's getting on his nerves to have them constantly jabbering away in that outlandish tongue, and it's high time they learned what's what.''

Both sisters laughed uncontrollably. Sydney slowed down the horses and wiped her eyes. "Oh, my heavens, that felt good. After last night I hadn't thought I'd ever laugh at anything again. But the absurdity of Littlecote turned tutor!'' They both went off into spasms for the second time. "And I suppose,'' she said when they'd somewhat recovered, "Lady Barbara is helping with the exercise?''

"No, actually.'' Mary Anne sobered up again. "I believe she's riding with Anthony. We shall likely see them by and by.''

"With her delightful auntie and Maxwell along, no doubt.'' The recent merriment was forgotten. Both sisters plunged back once more into their gloom.

Neither paid much attention to the approaching sound of carriage wheels, except that Sydney pulled her team over to allow the vehicle to pass. Instead, the high-perch phaeton matched its pace to theirs.

"Well, finally!" was Lord Linley Mortlock's greeting. "You really have developed into quite the little whip, m'dear. I've had the devil's own time catching up with you. Could you pull over there for just a bit?" He pointed toward a grassy verge. "For my pains, I'd like a word with you."

He halted his rig expertly behind them, climbed down from his perch, and handed the reins over to his tiger. Mary Anne was so busy drinking in his sartorial splendor—from the crown of his curly-brimmed beaver to the turned-down tops of his driving boots he was dressed entirely in white—that it took a moment for her eyes to focus upon his face. She gasped aloud. One eye was swollen shut; the skin around it was a vivid black-and-blue.

"What in the name of heaven has happened to you?" Sydney sounded more curious than concerned.

"Oh, but you should see the other cove" was the languid reply as he placed his white-gloved hands upon the curricle seat and gazed up at them.

"You in a mill? I'll not believe it."

He sighed. "I was afraid of that. So much for the sporting image. But you're right of course. You wouldn't catch me dead in Cribb's Parlor. Which is what I'd likely be if I attempted to do battle with any of the bruisers who frequent that barbaric place. No, what you see . . . ."—he gestured toward his battered face—"is not the result of any boxing mill. The fact is, I was scurvily attacked in my own house last night."

His eyes never left Sydney's face, for which Mary Anne could only be thankful since she herself would have had some difficulty looking him in the eye.

"You were what?" Sydney, of course, had no problem with sounding genuinely astonished.

"You heard me right. Attacked. Set upon. And I can't tell you, my dear Sydney, how relieved I am that you seem surprised. You see, I kept entertaining the teeniest suspicion that you might have had something to do with the incident."

Mary Anne was busily thanking her lucky stars she hadn't found the opportunity to tell her sister of Anthony's foray into the world of crime. Sydney was adept at hiding her emotions, but this situation could have sorely tried even her aplomb. As it was, her scornful laugh was genuine.

"You think I came to your house last night and attacked you? That blow to your face must have affected your brain. The notion's appealing, I'll admit. But too absurd."

Lord Linley's reply was aborted by a barouche filled with acquaintances that slowed in passing to bow in their direction. The passengers could be seen exchanging curious looks as they sped away.

"Well," he sighed, "I can see my battered phiz is going to be the *on dit* of London. I shall have to come up with a heroic tale to account for it."

"Something better than that I attacked you, I trust."

"Oh, I certainly never thought that, m'dear. I saw my attacker quite plainly, you see."

Mary Anne stiffened and just managed not to gasp.

"Besides the fact there was a bright moon shining," he explained, "the servants had left the candles burning for me."

"Well, then, at least you'll be able to describe your assailant," Sydney said. "You've reported it, I expect."

"Naturally I sent word to Bow Street right away. And they sent a villainous-looking fellow around. But as for describing the ruffian who assaulted me, I'm afraid that wasn't very helpful. His face was covered by a dark kerchief, don't you see. And he wore a stocking cap that hid his hair. So all I could tell the minion of the law was that the man was tall. He quite loomed over me in fact. Well-built and definitely muscular.'' He touched his cheekbone and winced.

"That, as they none too tactfully pointed out, was not a great deal to go on. Nor did it seem to help overly much," he added, "when I observed there was something oddly familiar about the cove. I'm almost certain the burglar was someone I know. But then," he shrugged, "I have such a broad acquaintanceship.''

"But surely not that broad," Sydney observed. "When did you start consorting with the common criminal?"

"That's the odd thing, Sydney darling. Somehow I don't believe this criminal was common in the least.''

"Whatever do you mean?"

"Well, for one thing, nothing was missing."

"Perhaps you surprised him before he had time to rob you."

"Perhaps. I doubt it, though. You see, I'm sure the fellow had been in my bedchamber."

"How could you tell?" Mary Anne blurted, then tried to look merely idly curious when for the first time Lord Linley took full notice of her.

"For one thing, the wardrobe door was left ajar, a state of affairs my valet would never allow to happen. Besides, it's only common sense to conclude that the burglar knew I'd be at Carlton House. No, I don't think he was any run-of-the-mill second-story man at all. What I do think, Sydney love, is that he came there looking for something in particular. Have I mentioned where he was when I surprised him?" He paused expectantly.

"Really, Linley, must you be so dramatic? All right, where was he?"

"In the picture gallery!"

"Is that supposed to be peculiar? As I recall, you've as many valuables there as anywhere."

"He did not come after the candelabras, Sydney." His good eye narrowed craftily to match the other's slit. "The thief was not even carrying a bag in order to make off with the silver and my jewelry. What he *was* doing when I happened on him was studying the paintings."

Mary Anne sensed that Sydney had grown wary. Her voice, however, remained nonchalant. "Since you are always prosing on about your art collection, the word must have traveled to the underworld that it's actually worth stealing."

"Oh, I think not," he purred. "I have a very valuable Holbein in my bedchamber he could have taken. But he didn't, don't you see."

"Oh, well then," she quipped, "perhaps he was simply an art lover who wished to browse."

"In my wardrobe? I think not. I'm sure he was looking for one particular painting. I'm also sure you're well aware of it, my dear Sydney."

"You're saying he came looking for my portrait, aren't you?"

"How very astute you are," he replied with heavy sarcasm.

"More so than you if you believe I had anything to do with your burglar. My acquaintanceship with the underworld is, unfortunately, quite limited. I can only wish, though, that your thief had been someone with that end in mind. I'd much rather have that odious painting wind up in some Parisian gallery than remain in your possession.

"But I'm sorry to say, Linley, your burglar was not working for me. Perhaps I should have hired someone to recover the thing, but the truth is, I've been convinced all along

*119*

you're merely toying with me for some reason of your own and mean to give the portrait back.''

He laughed at that. "You are indeed spoiled, aren't you, dear Sydney. You're accustomed to snapping your fingers and having men do anything you want—up to and including housebreaking, I've no doubt. But I don't succumb quite that easily. Your little scheme has ricocheted, in fact. For if I ever had considered returning that unclothed work of art, last night's episode would have quite changed my mind. To have suffered as I have done for art's sake . . .''—he touched his face gingerly—"is to make one's possession appear a pearl above price. No, I won't be giving that portrait up anytime soon, Lady Cunliffe.

"But I think it only fair to tell you what I have done. I've hired myself a thief-taker. That same Bow Street runner who came to investigate the break-in has agreed—for an outrageous sum that has increased the painting's value enormously—to patrol my premises and prevent another such occurrence. You should see the fellow, ladies. Regular monster of a man. A flattened nose. Ears like cabbages. An ex-pugilist, he says. I tell you all this by way of warning.''

"If you still believe I had anything to do with that business last night,'' Sydney raised her voice angrily, "well, you're madder than Old King George. And as for that tiresome portrait—'' The sound of approaching hooves caused her to bite off what she had been going to say.

Mary Anne looked behind them, and her blood ran cold. Anthony and Lady Barbara were galloping their way.

She prayed they'd merely nod and ride on by, but Lady Barbara, who was in the lead, pulled up her chestnut and greeted the party cordially. Anthony had no choice but to rein in his mount beside her.

Mary Anne tried to look anywhere but at his face. However, her eyes were drawn there as by a magnet, and her worst fears were confirmed. No miracle of healing had taken place. The scratches on his face were fierce and raw.

"Oh, I say, Captain," Lord Linley remarked casually after a bit of polite conversation, "what has happened to your face?"

"Funny you should ask." Anthony ran his fingers lightly over the scratches. "I was just wondering if it would be too untactful to ask you the same thing. Been in a mill, perhaps?"

"Not precisely. I was burglarized last night, and the thief attacked me."

Lady Barbara was quick to express her horror. Her probing questions led his lordship through a second recital of his harrowing experience. "After he had taken me·by surprise and hit me in that brutish fashion," he concluded, "my assailant jumped from the upstairs gallery window."

"Did he, by God!" Anthony exclaimed. "Pity the villain didn't break his neck."

He might have done," Lord Linley spoke deliberately, "except that the shrubbery broke his fall. Your face put me in mind of the whole fiasco. You see, one would suspect the culprit would have been quite scratched up by the contact."

"Bound to have been, I'd think."

"By the by, you still haven't said just how you came by your own markings."

"Oh, that." Captain Rodes made light of his minor injuries. "Nothing quite so dramatic as your own adventure, I'm afraid. My horse shied at a squirrel and ran me into a tree branch. Oh, but I say . . ." Anthony paused, frowned, and then began to look indignant. "Surely you aren't implying—"

"Don't be absurd, Anthony," Lady Barbara interjected. "Of course Lord Linley wasn't suggesting anything so absurd as that you scratched yourself upon his bushes. He was remarking upon the coincidence, that's all.

"But I must confess you've put me into quite a quake, Lord Linley. Until Lord Littlecote was saying so just the other day, I'd no idea how unsafe London has become. I do hope you are taking precautions, Lady Cunliffe. There are such lovely things in Cunliffe House. I should hate to think of a burglary."

"Oh, yes, do be warned, my dear Lady Cunliffe." Lord Linley's look was speaking. "From now on you should be very, very wary."

"Oh, I intend to be, Lord Linley. I most certainly intend to be."

After a bit more small talk, the gathering broke up. And for a while Sydney concentrated upon her driving. The crush had not abated; if anything, the traffic had grown heavier. Mary Anne held on to the carriage seat for dear life while doing her best not to think at all.

Not a word passed between the sisters until they'd safely navigated Hyde Park Corner and were pulling up in front of Cunliffe House. Then Sydney broke the silence. "I think it high time you and I sat down together and had a comfortable coze."

Some half hour later in her bedchamber Mary Anne sighed heavily at the end of a confession that had been dragged bit by bit from her sister over a pot of tea. "What a coil! Well, at least you can take one bit of consolation from it all. Anthony must truly love you to have put himself into such jeopardy. Or," she added sadly, "perhaps that's not a consolation since he's going to marry Lady Barbara."

"Oh, he didn't do it for me. He did it for Maxwell. He quite idolizes the general, you see."

"Everybody idolizes the general" was the dry rejoinder.

"But I'm afraid for Anthony. I should never have dumped

our troubles upon him. And now Lord Linley suspects." Her voice broke. "He could wind up in Newgate, and I'll be to blame."

"Oh come now. Let's not make more of a Cheltenham tragedy out of this than it is already. Linley might suspect, but there's no way to prove it. Just so long as Anthony gives up his life of crime—" She giggled suddenly. "Oh, lord, what would his reverend father say!"

Mary Anne groaned. "He'd know immediately it was all my fault. And I did so wish to make him proud of me."

Sydney looked at her curiously. "You really did, didn't you? Well, never mind. He'll not hear of it. We'll carry Anthony's guilty secret to our graves. And believe me, no one's going to Newgate over this."

Mary Anne's eyes suddenly widened in horror. "Oh, dear heaven, Mr. Wakley! I had forgot all about Mr. Wakley!" She crashed her teacup into her saucer. "I must warn him!"

"What on earth? Who is Mr. Wakley? Mary Anne, stop!" Sydney called out as her sister was in the act of dashing from the room. "What's put you into such a taking? Just who, for heaven's sake, is Mr. Wakley?"

"He's the one I hired to burgle Lord Linley's house. And he's the one who'll be nabbed by the thief-taker and blow the gaff about me if I don't find a way to head him off." The bedchamber door slammed behind her.

"Oh, dear God!"

Sydney sank back down weakly upon her chair and with a shaking hand poured out a fresh cup of reviving tea.

# Chapter
# Thirteen

*T*he Cunliffe household was having an evening at home.
No one, it seemed, had made any sort of social engagement for the night following the Prince Regent's fete. The consensus seemed to be that any outing following so closely upon the heels of that lavish entertainment could only prove anticlimactic to the extreme.

The residents had, perhaps, come to regret this decision, for dinner was by no means a festive occasion. For one thing, it had become impossible to ignore the icy politeness prevailing between the host and hostess. Even the Prussians seemed aware that all was not as it should be in that quarter. Lady Barbara and Captain Rodes stole frequent uneasy glances at Sir Maxwell and Lady Cunliffe throughout the meal. Lord Littlecote appeared bemused by the atmosphere.

Mary Anne was less distressed by the Cunliffe frigidity than by the sight of Anthony's marred and disapproving face.

Her mood kept swinging back and forth between a clammy-palmed horror of the terrible consequences had he been arrested and a seething anger at him for his assessment of her family's morals. Whichever way she vacillated, it made it very difficult to do the polite.

Oddly enough it was Lord Littlecote who finally managed to inject a slight degree of normalcy into the emotional turmoil dominating the dinner table. For once having set his hand upon the plow, his lordship was not the sort to consider looking back. Midway through the meal he seized upon the dining experience as an instructional resource for his tutorial in the English language.

Littlecote's course in practical usage consisted of first engaging the attention of the foreigners with some noisy, insistent throat clearing before loudly naming each separate item of food. This process, in a lavishly spread table, was a real time-consumer. At each remove his lordship would harrumph and then begin his catalog. "Potatoes," he would intone as he heaped a liberal portion upon his plate, and the Prussians would dutifully echo "Potatoes." "Partridge" he pronounced as his fork impaled one. The Prussians in unison repeated "Partridge." Then later, in review, Lord Littlecote, while chewing, would suddenly point his finger at a particular dish, and the Prussians would snap to and strive to identify it, thereby creating some confusion among the white-gloved footmen who leapt to serve the "fish" or "mutton" when it was named.

Mary Anne was soon diverted enough to laugh out loud at this novel English lesson, and even Sir Maxwell was seen to smile. Only Anthony, she observed, remained quite platter-faced. He ate sparingly of the multitudinous courses and replied to Lady Barbara's attempts at conversation as if he were being overcharged for every word.

But even so, by the end of the meal the mood was lighter.

And when Mary Anne happened to mention the waltz craze that was sweeping London, even Sydney entered the conversation to observe that since the shocking import from the Continent had actually been danced at Almack's it would behoove them all to master it.

The Prussians had been hanging upon their every word with studious intensity. Now the younger one made a valiant effort to enter the conversation. "You teached to us the English." He bowed toward Lord Littlecote. "Ve teach to you the valtz." His smile engaged them all.

This generous offer was greeted, if not enthusiastically, at least with gracious acquiescence. Learning to waltz would be one way to make it through an evening that could otherwise prove tedious to the extreme.

After the gentlemen had disposed of their port in record time, they rejoined the ladies in the drawing room, where the servants had rearranged the furniture and rolled up an Aubusson carpet to clear a dancing area. Lady Barbara and the Prussians immediately began an animated conversation in German while the others watched, rather warily. It was then up to Lady Barbara to pass on the conclusions of the consultation.

"Marshal Von Ziefen has consented to play for us." She smiled while the older Prussian endeavored to look modest. And, Sir Maxwell, if you will instruct your wife, Captain Rodes will—"

"I'm sorry, Lady Barbara," the general interrupted, "I hate to upset your plans, but I do not waltz."

"You don't?" She looked surprised. "But I had thought—" She broke off in some confusion. It was the first time Mary Anne had known her ladyship to be out of countenance.

"La, I own myself a bit surprised, too, sir," Sydney observed airily. "I had been led to believe that our military heroes on the Continent engaged in a social life that put us English provincials to shame.''

"I suspect you give yourself too little credit. From all reports the London social scene is unsurpassed.''

Well, so much for truce, Mary Anne thought. The emotions were swirling about the room once more.

"It is true,'' Sir Maxwell conceded, "that I have been in company where the waltz was danced. But as you may possibly have forgot, I seem to have two left feet where dancing is concerned.''

"That's odd. I remember you as a very graceful dancer.''

"But then perhaps you've confused me with someone else.'' The statement was a gauntlet flung between them.

"Perhaps. It does all seem quite a long time ago now.''

"Too long, it would appear.'' Then, after a pause, he added, "For me to recover such little dancing skill as I may once have possessed, I mean to say.''

"Well, never mind.'' Lady Barbara managed to pretend nothing out of the ordinary was happening. She smiled with an artificial brightness. "Count Roethke here will take Lady Cunliffe for his pupil; Captain Rodes will instruct Miss Hawtry.'' Anthony seemed about to speak, but then apparently changed his mind. "And I shall have the pleasure of instructing both you, Sir Maxwell, and Lord Littlecote.''

The general begged to be excused from the waltz lessons, however, on the grounds that he had some important letters he needed to write. His smile was rather forced, but he spoke lightly. "Composition makes a far more acceptable excuse than the fact I'm suddenly feeling my age among all you younger people.''

"Shall I send for a cane?'' Sydney murmured.

"No, thank you, m'dear. I'll stagger along the best I can and perhaps rejoin you later on for tea.''

"Well, now, shall we begin?'' Lady Barbara said brightly.

"First, it would be a good idea if Count Roethke and I danced a waltz for you." She quickly translated her suggestion to the young Prussian even though he'd evidently understood much of what she'd just said since he'd moved close beside her.

"Please observe our positions." She demonstrated by placing a gloved hand lightly upon the gentleman's shoulder while he clasped her about the waist.

"Don't look at all the thing." Lord Littlecote, who was standing beside Mary Anne, sniffed his disapproval.

"Would you prefer not to learn it, then?"

"Got to, don't you know. Been danced at Almack's." There was no arguing with that particular social dictum.

"You have to admit, though, it is quite pretty." Mary Anne, who had never seen the waltz danced before, was charmed by the graceful couple whirling before them. Their movements flowed together in perfect rhythm as they revolved beneath the sparkling prisms of the chandelier and were reflected back and forth in the narrow gilt-framed mirrors set within the pilasters that ranged along the walls. They smiled at each other, obviously pleased with their virtuoso performance. Mary Anne wondered if there was anything Lady Barbara did not do well.

"Goodness, just let me catch my breath a moment." Her ladyship fanned vigorously at the end of the demonstration. "Now, then, observe carefully," she said when she'd recovered. "It's quite simple, actually. *One*-two-three, *One*-two-three." She demonstrated the steps by herself once more. "Very well now. Let's all begin. If you will join your partners. Lord Littlecote, you're to dance with me."

Anthony did not exactly leap to her side, Mary Anne observed. In fact he looked as though he'd prefer to be almost anywhere but there.

"You don't have to do this, you know," she said beneath her breath.

"Oh, yes, I do" was the grim reply as, upon command, he took her in his arms.

It was unfortunate that at just this moment a discussion in German arose between Lady Barbara, poised with Lord Littlecote, and Count Roethke, holding Lady Cunliffe, that seemed to concern the proper tempo for beginners. Captain Rodes appeared to be in a quandary—whether to drop his partner like a hot potato or to hold his position as the others were doing.

"I do hope you aren't lusting after me," Mary Anne said sweetly.

"No danger." He glared down.

"I can't tell you how relieved I am to hear it, knowing your bent toward that sort of thing. But then of course you rather tend to blame your weaknesses upon someone else."

"All right. You've made your point," he growled into her ear. "I'm sorry for what I said—and did—last night. Now can we forget it?"

Marshal Von Ziefen at last struck a resounding chord upon the pianoforte, and the waltz began. Anthony hurled the two of them into the dance. "Ouch! Stay off my toe there, will you!"

"How can I help it if you jerk so? And you're supposed to be an expert! You should have paid more attention to the Prussian."

"Don't preach at *me*. You're the one who turned out to be cow-footed."

"There's no such term."

"There is now. You've just invented it. I beg your pardon." He'd collided with Lord Littlecote, who was grimly steering Lady Barbara.

"Really, Anthony, this is absurd," Mary Anne lectured

in an undertone. "We always used to dance excellently together."

"We never waltzed."

"Well, there's no reason it should be an exception. If only you'd stop treating the whole thing like a cavalry charge."

He grinned despite himself. "All right. I'll admit some fault. But pray remember that you'll have to allow *me* to lead *you*, which does run counter to your nature."

She sighed. "Really this is impossible. And I do wish to learn the waltz. Could you not simply pretend I am someone else?"

"If I could do that, life, and not just this dance, would be one hell of a lot simpler."

"Try, then."

But the music had stopped, and the opportunity was over.

Lady Barbara beamed her approval, toward one of the couples at any rate. "That was truly an excellent beginning. Lady Cunliffe, I will not believe you have never waltzed before. Now, then, Count Roethke, perhaps you could change partners and help Miss Hawtry master the steps. And, Anthony, why don't you partner Lady Cunliffe this time?"

During the second waltz, Mary Anne's performance improved prodigiously, the credit for which she was willing to lay at the feet of her instructor. So confident had she grown, in fact, that she shot a look of triumph toward the 'cowfooted' captain to underscore the fact that their recent ineptitude was all his fault. But she was unable to catch his eye. He and her sister were gliding around the floor in a harmony of movement that outdid even the graceful Prussian's recent partnering. Why, that clodpoll's actually a dab hand at the waltz, she thought viciously. "Oh, I do beg your pardon," Mary Anne apologized as she missed a step.

By the time she'd danced two more waltzes she was feeling quite confident in her ability to take the floor, even within the hallowed walls of Almack's. This confidence became a bit eroded, though, when Littlecote claimed her hand. She found his constant muttering of "*one*, two, three; *one*, two, three" a bit off-putting, and his movements too mechanical by half. Still, at the conclusion of the dance, she was able to share his enthusiasm though she confessed aloud it surprised her. "Why, yes, I do like the waltz above all dances. But I'd feared you might not."

"Why ever wouldn't I?"

"Well, you did seem to disapprove at first."

"Not a bit of it. It's like a breath of fresh air in fact. I've thought for years now that Almack's is far too stuffy. The waltz should liven things up there quite a bit."

Lord Littlecote's liberated view of the shocking new dance was shared by all the others. And when the tea board was brought in at the conclusion of the lesson, a lively discussion of the waltz's many social merits most fortunately kept the company occupied. For had there been any lull in the conversation, someone might have been tempted to remark upon the fact that their host, Sir Maxwell, had failed to join them for the spread.

# Chapter Fourteen

**"I've been giving the matter serious thought, and I think we should be married right away. As soon as the peace celebration is over, that is."**

The morning following the waltz lesson Lord Littlecote had cornered Mary Anne at breakfast and asked for a word with her. They had retired to the yellow drawing room for privacy. Mary Anne sat in a wing chair examining a picture in colored silks that someone had left on the worktable next to it while Littlecote paced back and forth, his brow furrowed with careful consideration of what he wished to say. Feeling ridiculously like a schoolgirl, Mary Anne prepared herself to receive a scold. But when he finally did get his thoughts in order, his words took her totally by surprise.

"Married right away! Don't talk fustian, Roderick. You cannot have let it slip your mind that our betrothal's at an end."

"No such thing. Hasn't been in the *Gazette*, now, has it?" He dared her to defy the logic of that statement.

"That's entirely beside the point. I'm not crying off with the *Gazette*, but with you. That is to say, it makes no difference—"

"Just listen a minute, will you," he interrupted. "Been giving the matter serious thought. And there it is. We should get married. Right away. Best thing for both of us." He had stopped his pacing and now stood looking down at her.

"Oh, really, Roderick." She felt at quite a disadvantage, craning her neck this way. But she tried to shake off the schoolgirl feeling and reason like an adult. "It amazes me you should talk this way. I'm certain you don't love me. In point of fact, I'm not convinced you even like me all that much. Why, I daresay," she fished, "you'd prefer the company of any number of women over mine. Let's take Lady Barbara—just as an example. You'd much rather be with her than me. Why not admit it?"

"So that's it!" The light of comprehension broke like sunrise upon his face. "By gad, you're jealous!" He sat down suddenly in a chair opposite hers and slapped his knee. "B'gad, jealous! You, of me! That does beat everything, and that's a fact. Never occurred to me you could be. You such a beauty and all. And me such an ordinary sort of cove. But then, I could never hope to understand how the female mind works."

"Don't talk such rubbish, Roderick. I am not jealous."

"Couldn't expect you to admit it. Well, there's no need to be. Lady Barbara's a prime 'un, no mistake, but it's sapskulled to get your nose out of joint because of her. She's betrothed, remember?"

"It simply never occurs to you that a betrothal can be broken."

"Well, it does happen," he conceded. "But it ain't at all

the thing. Besides," he pointed out reasonably, "Captain Rodes is quite plump in the pocket, I understand, as well as being a military hero. And he could even be termed handsome, I collect. Females take to that sort of thing, you see. So why on earth should Lady Barbara wish to cry off?"

The question was certainly a poser.

"But, dash it, Mary Anne, I really wish you wouldn't get me off the subject. For Lady Barbara has nothing to say in the matter. The thing is—and it's the only thing—you and I will deal famously."

"We will do nothing of the sort."

"Now, there's no need to take that tone with me, miss. I know it's a bit much to expect a female who fancies herself in love to use her head, but you should at least make an effort. The fact of the matter is, he'll never marry you."

"I'm well aware of that," she answered miserably.

"So there we are!" He might have just jumped her king. "That's my point. The sooner you marry me the better, don't you see."

"But I've told you all along I don't love you, Roderick."

"I know." He impatiently waved her objection away. "And a very good thing, too, I'd call it, given the type of cove you do fall in love with."

"And just what do you mean by that?" She bristled.

"Oh, I've been making some inquiries. And everyone says the same. The man's a scoundrel. Yes, I know he's Sir Maxwell's cousin, but, still, there it is. Besides which—well, there's all sorts of tittle-tattle circulating about him and Lady Cunliffe. And how you could fancy yourself in love with a man who's having an affair with your own sister is beyond any understanding, Mary Anne. It don't speak highly of you, and that's a fact. But there it is, and, well, I'm prepared to blink at it."

"That's certainly noble of you."

"Yes, it is for a fact."

"Roderick!" With difficulty she got her anger under control and attempted to speak reasonably. "I was merely being sarcastic. Please, please, do get that maggot out of your head. I am not in love with Lord Linley. The idea's not just absurd, it's disgusting. And I'm sorry now that I ever said I was in love with anybody. For the only point at issue is this—and let me say it for the final time—Roderick, we would not suit."

"That's where you're wrong." His face glowed with triumph. "Been trying to tell you. We'd suit to a tee. And for heaven's sake don't start up again about not loving me. I know all that. And you're right, most likely, that I don't love you either. I couldn't say as to that since I've never been sure exactly what people mean in that regard. But I do know we'd suit. Wasn't too sure of it down in Bath. Don't mind saying now that I was having a lot of second thoughts, what with Mama's disapproval and all. But coming to London was the smartest thing we could have done, and I'm obliged to you for thinking of it. Yes, it was damned clever of you to lure me up here."

"To what?" she choked. "I never—"

"Well, maybe not intentionally. But if you'd stopped to think about it—well, never mind. What I'm trying to tell you," he spoke humbly, "is I don't think I've ever enjoyed myself as much as I have here. Didn't like London above half any other time, you see. Couldn't wait to leave the place. But this has been altogether different. Being here in Sir Maxwell's house—in the thick of things. Something going on all the time. Meeting the cream of society. Going to Carlton House. Makes a cove feel like the very pink of the *ton*, I can tell you. Being Sir Maxwell Cunliffe's sister more than makes up for not bringing me a fortune." They were both much too intent upon what he was saying to notice the door opening.

"And I know when you stop and really think on it, you'll have to see that the advantage of marrying me outweighs any other—er—consideration in your mind. And now *I* can see how you might have hated the idea of rusticating. Well, I'll put your mind to rest on that score, Mary Anne. I'm planning to bring my town house up to scratch for you. We'll live in London the best part of every year."

"Please forgive the intrusion." A dry voice spoke from the doorway. "Lady Barbara has left her tambouring in here, and I've come to fetch it."

Just why Anthony's gaze should cause Mary Anne's face to flame was beyond her understanding. Certainly his expression revealed no clue as to how long he'd been standing there.

"Oh, my word!" Lord Littlecote's gaze had fastened upon the ormolu clock adorning the mantelpiece. "Supposed to see my man of business at eleven. Want to talk to him about having my house done over. Pray excuse me, m'dear." And he bent formally over Mary Anne's hand. "Captain." He nodded toward Anthony as he hurried from the room.

Anthony walked toward the worktable, and Mary Anne wordlessly handed him the needlework and silks.

"I see congratulations are in order. Once again. I'm flattered you took my advice to heart about patching things up with Lord Littlecote. You really are a credit to your sex, Miss Hawtry. Not even to mention your illustrious family. You've got the poor widgeon eating out of your hand again."

"Go to the devil, Anthony."

"No, Miss Hawtry. That's exactly what I do not intend to do."

"Oh, you're reformed, all right," she was goaded into sneering. "You're a regular tame lapdog in fact. Fetching needlework like any good old Rover. Do you also roll over and beg?"

"You won't make me rise to bait, Mary Anne."

This seemed to be her morning for having males loom over her. She wished to stand and assert herself, but her knees had betrayed her by going weak. Why it could not be her mouth instead that became afflicted in Anthony's presence was quite incomprehensible.

"Believe me," he glared down upon her, "I can't tell you how refreshing it is to do harmless little errands like 'fetching' needlework. I'll admit it calls for a bit of adjustment to grow accustomed to the fact that my fiancée has no desire for me to take up a life of crime, with the choice of either breaking my fool neck or winding up in Newgate. But I'm looking forward more than I can say to growing accustomed to that state of affairs."

"Well, there's no need to rub it in. I already know just how superior Lady Barbara is to me."

"Good."

"There is just one thing, though, you tend to overlook in all of your odious comparisons."

"Oh, really? And what might that be?"

"That I'm the one you're actually in love with."

For a moment she had the satisfaction of knowing she'd landed him a leveler. But the satisfaction was short-lived. In an instant he was figuratively back up on his feet.

"I wouldn't be too sure of that, Miss Hawtry. And even if it should happen to be the case—which, mind you, I'm certainly not admitting—you know what they say about that particular malady. Being in love, I mean. The affliction is most generally of a temporary nature. In point of fact, the recovery rate is staggering, I'm told. So my own prognosis for a speedy recovery is excellent. Your servant, Miss Hawtry." He bowed elaborately in her direction, gave the tambouring a toss from one hand to the other, and started toward the door.

"Oh, Anthony," she called after him in a small, pathetic voice.

He turned reluctantly.

"I wish you happy." Her voice broke. "I really, truly mean it."

"Like hell you do!" he snarled as the door slammed shut behind him.

Causing Anthony to lose his temper after he'd bested her so devastatingly in their verbal duel was a petty victory. But it was all she had for the moment, so it would have to do. Mary Anne sat and savored it for a while.

# Chapter
# Fifteen

As the house party set out toward Hyde Park soon after dark, Mary Anne reflected that the only members of the group in a proper festive mood were Miss Savannah Cunliffe and Lord Roderick Littlecote.

And at that, there was some confusion in the toddler's mind about the outing, since Hyde Park was synonymous in her mind with ducks. It had taken a bit of persuasion to get her to leave the house without a supply of bread. "You can't blame the child for being mixed-up." Her father sighed after trying to explain they were going to witness a naval battle. "I don't half believe it myself."

"By Jove, a regular Battle of Trafalgar taking place upon the serpentine!" Lord Littlecote exclaimed. "That really should be something to tell our grandchildren."

The last part of his remark was directed toward Mary Anne. For some unaccountable reason, her face flamed red.

"A third generation of little Littlecotes. Now, there's a picture for you," Captain Rodes, walking behind them, remarked sotto voce. Lady Barbara looked at him intently.

Sir Maxwell and Lady Cunliffe walked side by side with Savannah riding on her father's shoulders. The baby's chatter helped to cover the fact that, except when necesity dictated, the parents seldom spoke to each other. And then their remarks were pared down to the bare essentials.

Mary Anne was preoccupied with her many problems. In a less heroic type, Captain Rodes's demeanor might have been described as sulking. Lady Barbara, usually the one to salvage a social situation, had withdrawn within herself. Even the Prussians were responsive to the atmosphere and seemed unusually subdued. It was a pity they could not all adopt Lord Littlecote's and Savannah's eagerness for an entertainment billed as the highlight of these many weeks of celebration.

For the Prince Regent was most anxious that none of his subjects be excluded from the peace festivities. Hence he had given orders that, beginning August first, great celebrations should be held in Hyde Park, St. James's Park, and Green Park, with access to all.

The immediate result of his good intentions had been to change the character of Hyde Park completely, a fact that the residents of Cunliffe House, along with other members of the *ton*, had reason to deplore. "Between the bareness and the tents we might be headed now for a desert oasis," Sir Maxwell remarked to the group at large as they wove their way through the gathering crowd.

It was true that the sands of Arabia did easily spring to mind as they walked upon the dry and crumbling soil where the tramping of thousands of feet had destroyed the last vestiges of green. But the booths and tents that edged the waters in a two-mile circle were a far cry from bedouin and camel.

The union jack fluttered proudly over the majority of them. Players and circus acts pranced upon their temporary stages. Souvenir trinkets were for sale everywhere, as were the usual light refreshments, now with unusual names: Jubilee nuts, Regent cakes, Royal Alexander gingerbread.

But the most numerous tents by far were those devoted to refreshment of the liquid sort. Publicans from London, Westminster, Marylebone, and miles beyond had shifted their kegs, bottles, corkscrews, foodstuffs, and waiters into the park. Whole alehouses, with the exception of their outer shells, had set up shop along the serpentine. The rural beauty of the place had completely disappeared, along with its fresh air. Liquor fumes, cheap tobacco, and, most prevalent of all, the collective bodies of dirty people, fouled the atmosphere. "Phew!" was Sydney's reaction as they weaved their way through the crowds and she applied a perfumed handkerchief to her nose.

Yet the excitement of the crowd, never mind its social background, was contagious. And the sight of small Savannah, waving a newly purchased flag above her father's head while shouting loud huzzahs, brought smiles to even the most stubbornly set faces in the Cunliffe group. Then, too, the general bearing the adorable little girl upon his shoulders was often recognized, despite the fact that he was not in uniform. "God bless 'e, sir!" was a frequent greeting. On more than one occasion small knots of people broke into raucous cheers. Mary Anne had been completely out of charity with her sister's husband since she'd witnessed the illicit embrace at Carlton House. But she now grudgingly admired the fact that Maxwell seemed more embarrassed than puffed up by all this adulation.

A little later, the group had reason to be grateful for the hero's popularity. For just as they'd despaired of finding a spot where they could view the sham naval battle, someone at the rear of the crowd shouted "Make room for the general" and the throng parted like a Red Sea composed of human beings and allowed them to slip through to the very water's edge.

At first, Miss Savannah Cunliffe enjoyed the re-created conflict, clapping her hands at all the pretty ships with their tall masts, white sails, and flags fluttering in the breeze. But soon the roar of cannon made her press her hands upon her ears, and when one of the "enemy" burst into flames, she screamed in terror.

"Here, let me," Anthony whispered when the general was about to take his daughter away. "These folk gave up their places on your account."

As she was being transferred from one broad set of shoulders to another, Savannah was just about to object to the substitution until Mary Anne assured her, "It's all right. I'll go, too." This may have earned her a dark look from Anthony, but it effectively cut off the tears in small Savannah's eyes.

They edged their way through the crowd and on past the row of tents and booths to a wooden bench underneath a tree where one of the myriad lanterns that illuminated the park was hung.

Anthony transferred Savannah from his shoulder to his lap, and Mary Anne gently removed the child's fingers from her ears. "There now, sweetheart. It's not nearly so noisy back here."

"And they weren't really shooting at one another, you see," Anthony reassured her. "It was just pretend. Nothing but noise and smoke."

"Go boom!" Savannah announced with disapproval.

"There'll be fireworks in a bit, and you'll like that much, much better than the battle."

And sure enough, when a brilliant blaze of rocketry announced the triumph of Britannia over the scurrilous French, the child was enraptured. She clapped her hands and squealed with delight as a shower of multicolored stars temporarily adorned the darkened skies.

Between watching the pyrotechnic spectacle and observing her niece's reaction to it, Mary Anne was so diverted that she failed to notice a repeated ''hist! hist!'' that kept up somewhere behind them until Anthony muttered ''What the devil!'' and she followed his gaze to spy a figure standing in the shadows beckoning. ''Hist!'' it repeated loudly. ''Hist, Miss Hawtry!''

''That ruffian's actually calling your name.'' Anthony frowned. ''Here, you take Savannah. I'd better look into this.''

''Oh, no! That isn't necessary.'' She was already on her feet. ''I know him. It's quite all right, I can assure you.''

''Just the same, I'm coming with you.''

''And have Savannah miss the fireworks? I should say not.''

The captain was obviously torn as to where his duty lay. But a squeal from the child in response to a fiery whirligig tilted the balance. ''Then you stay where I can see you,'' he ordered. ''Or else I'll be there.''

''Well, it's about time,'' Mr. Ned Wakley complained when Mary Anne had arrived within earshot. ''I've been 'alf histing meself 'oarse.''

''Well, why didn't you simply walk over to where we were?'' she asked reasonably.

''And get picked up by the Charlies? You think I'm dicked in the nob or something? The place is fair crawling with 'em.'' He had faded back into the foliage once again, whereas Mary Anne, mindful of Anthony's imperative, remained well out in the open. To a curious passerby she might have been conversing with a bush.

"Well, I see no reason for us to be chatting anyhow," she said. "We've no need for further dealings."

"The devil you say!" the bush exploded. "The 'further dealings' we 'ave is for you to pay me wot I've got rightfully coming. That's the 'further dealings' we've got a need for. And the quicker you cough up the blunt the better, for I don't mind saying this 'ere park's too 'ot for me by 'alf."

"What I owe you!" Her voice rose. "Why I don't owe you anything. I sent round a note calling off our—er—business arrangement. You may keep the sum I advanced, however," she added magnanimously.

"Now see 'ere, miss. I was 'ired to break and henter and break and henter's wot I done. And for me pains I ran smack into Nick Stubbs, the biggest, meanest bruiser Bow Street's ever spawned. And I can tell you right now if it 'adn't been for the rotten stitching in me collar and the fact there was an open window a foot away—and 'ow I kept from breaking every bone in me body when I jumped Gawd only knows—well, I'd be gallows bait by now. And soon may be anyhow if you don't cough up me wages and let me get back to Covent Garden."

"But I called the whole thing off!" she protested. "I knew Lord Linley had hired a thief-taker to watch his paintings. That's why I wrote the note to warn you away. Don't tell me you didn't see it. My footman said he took it to the coffee shop and the proprietor told him he'd make sure you got it. Don't tell me he never gave it to you!"

"Oh, I got it, right enough. But that's not to say I read it."

"Why ever not?" She glared, then added on second thoughts, "Oh, of course. I see. But then why on earth didn't you ask somebody else to read it to you?"

"Didn't see the need of it. Figured you were just reminding me unnecessarily of our arrangement. Which I followed through on. And now I want me blunt.''

"Did you get the painting?"

It was all Mary Anne could manage not to stick her fingers in her ears, à la Savannah, at the exploded stream of epithets. "No, I didn't get the painting! I just explained why not. You let me walk into a trap set with Bow Street runners and now I expect full payment." The little ferret's voice had a dangerous edge.

"I only agreed to pay if you got the painting." Mary Anne had started to edge away when a dirty paw snaked out of the bushes and clamped onto her wrist. "Besides, I don't have the money with me," she protested as she tried to pull away.

"Well, then we can just take those sparklers I spy winkin' under your bonnet brim, then, can't we?"

"No, we can't!" She gave her arm a jerk that nearly pulled it from its socket with no resulting easing of his grip. "They aren't my earrings. They're my sister's."

"So's the picture. Now there's justice for you. 'And 'em over!"

But at this juncture Mr. Wakley came flying from the bush, propelled by Anthony's grasp upon his arm, which was still clamped like a vise on Mary Anne's. As a result, she was almost spun right off her feet.

"Unless you want your claret drawn, let go of the lady."

Mr. Wakley did so with a howl.

"Now, then, do I call the Charlies or do you move on and quit bothering Miss Hawtry?"

A look of cunning made the burglar's face more rodent-like. "Oh, I don't think you'll do that, guv."

The most probable reason Captain Rodes did not answer right away was that he was studying the fresh scratches on the other's face intently. Their pattern might have been a copy of the tracery of his own. Mr. Wakley took advantage of this conversational lull to press his point.

"And wot might prevent you from turning me over to the law, you're thinking? Well, now, I'll tell ye wot. They'll find it wery, wery peculiar down at Bow Street when I tell 'em as 'ow this 'ere lady 'ired me to commit a crime. That's why you won't turn me over to the Charlies, guv."

Miss Hawtry was massaging her tender wrist while anxiously gazing toward the bench where Savannah lay asleep. The captain gave her a long, assessing look. "Mary Anne, I won't even bother to ask you what this is all about."

"Would be a waste of time right enough, guv," Mr. Wakley offered. "String you some pack of lies she would, now, wouldn't she? Butter wouldn't melt in her mouth most likely. Lamb-innocent she seems. But the gospel truth is, this 'ere hinnocent young lady 'ired me to lift a certain painting. Of her sister, so she says. But if it ain't 'erself wot's been painted starkers, well, then, I'm a Dutchman. She promised me three hundred pounds to do the job, and I want me blunt. Plus a ten pound bonus for 'azardous duty," he added. " 'Safe as 'ouses,' that's wot she told me. 'Everyone'll be in the park,' she says. Wot she didn't say was that Nick Stubbs'd be lurkin' there to nab me the minute I stepped inside the place."

After a lengthy silence, the captain reached inside his coat and produced a purse.

"But he didn't get the painting," Mary Anne protested.

Anthony didn't spare her a glance as he transferred money into a dirty, outstretched palm. "Be off with you now," he ordered.

"Twenty pounds! You must be funning! Or deaf, more likely. The fee agreed on was three hundred."

"That was for success. You failed. Now be off with you."

"Well, it wasn't my fault I failed, now, was it?" The burglar held his ground. "Besides, that ain't the point, now, is it? For it ain't the picture we're dickering over right now, if you take me meaning, guv'nor. It's the lady's good name wot's become the merchandise. For just supposin' you was to be so cruel and inhuman as to turn me over to the law, and then I wuz to tell 'em down at Bow Street that this refined young female gentry-mort hactually 'ired me to snitch one of Lord Linley's pictures. Wot do you suppose they'd be thinking then?''

The captain refused to acknowledge Mary Anne's clutch upon his sleeve. "Why, that you're a liar, naturally."

"That's as may be," the other sneered.

"That's as would be. Whose word are they likely to take—yours or this angelic-looking lady's?"

"I got truth on me side." Mr. Wakley endeavored to look virtuous.

"But she's got breeding. Not at all fair, I'll grant you, but there it is. It's an unfair world."

"Well, 'er name'd be blackened all the same."

"Do you really think Miss Hawtry would care for that?"

The little thief was rapidly beginning to deflate. "No, I expect not," he muttered. "Any female who'd be painted wearing no more clothes than Mother Eve ain't likely to have any good name to lose."

"Well then, there you are. So be reasonable. Twenty pounds is nothing to sneer at, you know. Don't try to pretend you do better than that most evenings, for I won't believe you. And as the lady pointed out, it's not as if you delivered up the goods. So look at the bright side. You weren't caught and you're twenty pounds ahead. All in all, not a bad night's work. So be off with you. And don't bother this lady again."

"Oh, you needn't worry about that, guv." Mr. Wakley shot a venomous look at Miss Hawtry. "I don't ever plan to 'ave any more dealings with 'er kind. Stick to me own sort from now on I will where a cove can know wot's wot." With a parting nasty scowl, Mr. Wakley disappeared into the bushes.

Mary Anne breathed a long, heartfelt sigh of relief. "Oh, thank you, Anthony," she said.

# Chapter
# Sixteen

*He wheeled upon her viciously. "You little ninnyhammer.*
You numskull. You pea-goose—" he sputtered.

"No need to ring a peal over me." She clung to her dignity. "I realize I did a foolish thing."

"Do you?" His voice was bitter as they walked slowly toward the sleeping child. "I doubt you have the faintest notion of the kind of man you were dealing with."

"Well, I certainly had some idea," she retorted, "after seeing those horrible wretches in Wych Street."

"You went to Wych Street?" He looked appalled. "Who went with you?"

"Why, nobody. Well, that is to say I took a hackney. And there was this very nice jarvey who waited outside."

He groaned and struck his forehead with an open hand. "Mary Anne, you should be locked up in Bedlam. Straitjacketed, in fact. You should not be allowed to wander loose. You're a menace to yourself—to society.''

She was growing rather more than a bit nettled. ''Just what was I supposed to do, pray tell?'' she whispered as they approached the bench where Savannah was asleep. ''I had to get the painting back. And I'd certainly no notion *you'd* try and steal the thing.''

''For God's sake, lower your voice.''

''It is lowered. If it got any lower, it wouldn't exist.''

''Exactly.''

Perhaps it was an excess of guilt that made her lash out at him. ''And how dare you tell that, that thieving little weasel I cared nothing for my good name? You implied I was no better than a—than a lightskirt!''

''Well, what was I supposed to do, invite him to blackmail you for the rest of your life?'' He was carefully picking up the sleeping child.

''No, I guess not,'' she admitted grudgingly. ''But you didn't have to be quite so convincing. You sounded as if you actually believed—''

''Let's drop the subject. Come on, the others will be wondering what's happened to us.'' He began walking swiftly toward the appointed meeting place, weaving his way skillfully in and out among the milling crowd while Mary Anne struggled to keep up.

''Of course I'll pay you back the money you gave Mr. Wakley.''

''Damn the money,'' he flung back into her teeth. ''I don't give two figs about the money. I just wish to God I didn't have to worry about you getting some new maggot in your brain.''

''Oh, you mean you actually do worry about me?'' She brightened up.

''Let's just say I worry about all the poor innocents whose

lives you turn arsy-varsy. I even admit to a certain sympathy for that snake Wakley. Brothers under the skin, he and I, when it comes down to it.''

She was still searching for a proper set-down when they reached a tent with a sign proclaiming GOOD FARE IS HERE and saw the rest of their party seated alfresco at a large round table.

"What kept you?" Sydney called out as they approached. "We were getting worried."

"A conversation with an acquaintance," Anthony replied evasively as he transferred the sleeping child to her mother's lap. He then went over to sit next to Lady Barbara, who'd broken off a conversation with Lord Littlecote to greet them. The Prussians rose politely. The younger one took a deep breath and remarked, "Much persons in the park, yah?"

"Oh, yes indeed," Mary Anne replied. "I do believe there's not a soul left in London who *isn't* at the park."

And as though to prove her point Lord Linley Mortlock came strolling by at that very moment and gave an exaggerated start of surprise at the sight of them. "Well, I must say that you're a sight for sore eyes indeed. I'd begun to believe the place was awash with nothing but cits. The smell alone is enough to make one long for continual war if this is what peace brings down upon our heads." He waved toward the passing parade and shuddered.

"I'm surprised to see you here among the rabble," Sir Maxwell said as his cousin prepared to join them uninvited. He moved his chair over to make room for Linley at the table.

"You're actually drinking ale?" His lordship eyed the mug Sir Maxwell held and shook his head. "How very egalitarian of you. But to reply to your comment, of course I'm here, dear boy. Needn't think you military coves are the only patriots. I became especially patriotic when the Duke of Clarence invited me to be one of his party." He waved away the sliced ham his cousin proffered with a wrinkling of his aristocratic nose. "There's supper afterward, thank God. Suppose I'll have to go to the old boy's house alone, though. No hope of finding them in this crush."

"You're probably right, Lord Linley," Lady Barbara offered. "Miss Hawtry and Captain Rodes became separated from the rest of us and we despaired of ever seeing them again, despite the fact we'd set a meeting place."

"Oh, really?" Lord Linley turned his quizzing glass toward the two and the captain looked slightly disconcerted. Mary Anne shot a quick look at Lady Barbara. But if there was any hidden barb in her observation, her pleasant expression did not reveal it.

"Well, now, I'm more than pleased that the fates or whatever have brought us all together," Lord Linley said, "for I particularly desire this meeting on two accounts. First, I have news. Sydney, m'dear, you will be especially interested since you know about my harrowing experience of a few nights ago. Well, a similar occurrence took place at my house this evening. I'd gone home, you see, to change my coat. Some oaf had jostled against me and smeared mustard on my sleeve."

"How ghastly for you." Lord Littlecote did not trouble to disguise his sneer.

"Why, yes it was, actually." Lord Linley's level stare caused Littlecote to redden. "But as it happened, my arrival back home was most opportune. I found everything there at sixes and sevens." He paused dramatically. "I'd been visited by another burglar, you see."

He waited till the gasps and exclamations of his listeners subsided and then continued. "It does give one furiously to think, does it not? Why should I, of all people, suddenly become the favorite target for thieves? Now if the underworld were converging upon Cunliffe House . . ."—he smiled mechanically at his cousin—"that would be understandable. Now, there's a regular treasure trove. But since I'm known to be a man of humble means—"

"Doing it rather brown, aren't you, Cousin?"

"All thing are, of course, relative. I certainly don't claim to be precisely poor. Still, it does make one stop and wonder just why I should be singled out by the criminal element for so much attention. The more I dwell on it, in fact, the more I'm convinced it's not a happenstance. I conclude that I possess some item someone wants desperately."

Lady Barbara's eyes were wide. "But have you no clue as to what that might be?"

"Actually, there is one thing. On both occasions the thieves were discovered in the picture gallery."

"Don't tell me you've a Rembrandt on your wall." Sir Maxwell signaled to the waiter for more ale.

"Oh, no, nothing of the kind. You must know if anything of that sort had existed in our family, it would have gone to you." There was just a trace of acid in Lord Linley's voice. He seemed to realize the fact, for he quickly smiled and shrugged. "No, alas, I have no old masters that I'm aware of."

"Maybe one's hidden away beneath a more modern canvas," Mary Anne theorized. "I've heard of such."

"Have you indeed? What a lovely thought. But no, I can't convince myself the thieves would be quite so fanciful."

"You keep saying 'thieves,' " Lady Barbara observed. "You're sure the first one didn't come back again?"

"I'm positive. The man from Bow Street whom I'd hired to guard the house—quite a waste of money as it turned out; he was no better at collaring an intruder than I was—said this was a little, weasely sort of fellow, whereas the one who attacked me was a tall, athletic type."

"You're sure you didn't exaggerate his size?" Lord Little-cote's contempt again shone through.

"Quite sure. But I'm not so certain the two weren't in collusion. Their modus operandi, if that's the proper phrase, was amazingly similar. Both jumped out the very same window. Both must have been scratched by the bushes underneath." His eyes wandered to the captain's face, but that military gentleman appeared to take no notice. "I can tell you I was not at all pleased with my Bow Street hireling. Gave him a good tongue-lashing for not seeing to it that the window was shut and bolted. He had the nerve to complain that the house was stifling. As if I were paying him good money to stay cool!

"Well, enough of those adventures. Let me get on to the second reason this meeting is fortuitous. I wish to invite you all to take a late supper with me tomorrow night in St. James's Street. Who knows, maybe our thief—the weasely one I mean—will show up again and enliven the proceedings. And if I can't precisely guarantee that sort of entertainment, Cousin, I can assure you I have the best chef in London. French of course. Fled the Corsican monster a few years back."

Sir Maxwell did his polite best to wriggle out of the invitation, claiming fatigue from all the celebrating. "Besides, we've made plans to watch the Green Park fireworks from our roof. It's the perfect vantage point, you know."

"Splendid! I'll simply join you there and we'll go on to my house later. I won't be fobbed off, you know. For one thing, the family would quite fail to understand it if I did not rise to the occasion and welcome our hero back." His eyes narrowed just a bit. "God knows how many other wills I might be written out of. But don't disturb yourself, Cousin. I can certainly sympathize with your fatigues. Being lionized is, no doubt, quite wearying. But you'll be subjected to none of that tomorrow evening. I'm not planning a party, you understand. Oh, dear no. I simply plan to dine *en famille.* Just those of us here.'' His eyes scanned the table and landed on the Prussians. "I collect we must include our mute foreign friends. Pray do pass on my invitation. And, oh, yes,'' he added as if in afterthought, "I have asked Mrs. Edleston to join us. She could be considered family, wouldn't you say?'' He smiled slyly. "I refer, of course, to the fact that she is our Lady Barbara's aunt.''

Sydney had stiffened at his words. Mary Anne was longing to throttle him. General Maxwell, however, did not change expression. "I am sorry, Cousin, to upset your plans. Some other time perhaps.''

"How unlike you to be so rag-mannered, Maxwell.'' Sydney's smile was brittle. Two bright spots burned in her cheeks. "Of course we'd be delighted to take supper with Linley. Who could resist the lure of a French chef *and* Mrs. Edleston?'' She looked round the table. "It's agreed, then? Good!'' Before anyone could speak she had answered her own question. "And we'll all convene on our rooftop just before midnight for fireworks. I quite look forward to it, I must say.''

Mary Anne also looked forward to it. But in her case it was with deep foreboding. She could only hope that the Green Park pyrotechnic display would be the only fireworks on the docket for that evening.

# Chapter Seventeen

When Mrs. Edleston arrived with Lord Linley at Cunliffe House the following night, Sydney was every inch the gracious hostess. If there was any fault to be found in her conduct, it was that she was perhaps a bit too animated, her laugh too artificial, her gaiety rather forced as they drank their tea in the striped drawing room. And when they had finished, Mary Anne could not see the need for her to ask Sir Maxwell to personally escort Mrs. Edleston up the narrow stairway that took them to the roof.

Still it was preferable to the other alternative—that Sydney should suddenly transform into a fishwife and snatch handfuls of the black hair that showed beneath Mrs. Edleston's white satin turban. This was what Mary Anne herself longed to do when that lady claimed to have a great fear of heights and clung like a limpet to Sir Maxwell's arm as the party approached the marble balustrade that both ornamented and guarded the front section of the roof.

"We should be able to see quite well from here." Sir Maxwell made every effort to underplay the awkwardness of his position. "Of course we won't be able to get the full effect. I'm afraid we'll simply have to imagine the metamorphosis of Prinny's castle."

One of the conceits planned for the evening's celebration was a hundred-foot-high Castle of Discord that had been erected in Green Park and had become the object of much gawking and speculation. The allegorical intention was that after it had endured the horrors of fire and destruction, the edifice would explode at midnight and, once the smoke had cleared, leave behind—if all went well—a revolving Temple of Concord. This had been the Regent's own invention.

"By George, I wouldn't mind seeing that." Lord Littlecote spoke a bit regretfully.

"You're sure it isn't the Vestal Virgins you'd like to see?" Lord Linley mocked. "Understand they're to wear transparent draperies. That, too, is our Prinny's doing, so I've been told."

"I was not thinking of that at all," Littlecote retorted huffily. "Indeed I've heard of no such thing."

"How on earth can they explode one temple without destroying another?" Lady Barbara quickly asked.

The only person who seemed to have the faintest notion was the younger Prussian, who launched into a spate of German that left only Lady Barbara—perhaps—the wiser.

It did center the attention upon him, however, which gave Mary Anne the opportunity to approach Lord Linley. "I'd like a word with you, sir," she whispered.

"You would?" he murmured back. "Am I to find that flattering?"

He followed her across the roof in the semidarkness. His

eyebrows rose as she stepped behind a concealing chimney pot. "How very cloak-and-daggerish you're being." He still kept his voice low. "Or do I perhaps mistake the matter and this is actually an amorous assignation? Oh, well then. No need to look like that. One could always hope."

"Will you spare me your playacting, Lord Linley. The last thing in the world you desire is an amorous assignation with me. What I wish to know is, what are you really up to?"

"I'm sure I've no idea what you mean."

"Yes, you have. Bringing Mrs. Edleston here to flaunt in Sydney's face. If that's not mischief-making of the most despicable kind, then I don't know what is."

" 'Mischief-making'? I would not so term it. But then it's all in the point of view, isn't it? I did feel the mix would make for a diverting evening. So I'll plead guilty to that much. For it's so important, is it not, to achieve the proper alchemy among guests if a party's to be successful. It's even more important in a small group like this than in a large one. But you are wrong on one count. It wasn't that I wished to flaunt Mrs. Edleston in Sydney's face. It was Max's reaction to having his wife and mistress cheek to jowl that I longed to see. But, as usual, my cousin disappoints me. I should have known better than to expect full value from such a contretemps. After all, my cousin's coolness under fire is legendary."

"I say, what's going on here?" an indignant voice hissed behind them. Lord Littlecote loomed in the shadows.

"Nothing's going on," Mary Anne replied. "I simply need to speak privately to Lord Linley on a personal matter."

"No, you don't. There's nothing personal you can possibly say to this jackanapes."

"Oh, come now, sir. It's one thing to be jealous, quite

another to be offensive, don't you know." Lord Linley sounded less offended than amused, however.

"Jealousy's got nothing to say in the matter. By Jupiter, it don't look right for my fiancée to be skulking behind chimney pots with a cove of your reputation."

"Oh, well then. When you put it like that, I accept your apology." Lord Linley helped himself to snuff.

"Apology!" his lordship sputtered. "You think I'm apologizing? I'll have you know—"

"Really, Roderick, you're being most absurd." Mary Anne stepped in to stem the tide.

"I am not. And it's high time you learned what's what. My mother was right about that much at least when she said neither you nor your sister care a fig for appearances."

"We do, too!" Mary Anne flung back, forgetting to keep her voice down. "We are simply not going to live our lives for small-minded people who insist upon casting the most commonplace behavior in the worst possible light."

"It ain't commonplace to skulk behind chimney pots."

"Now, now, children." Lord Linley spoke mock-soothingly. "We are beginning to attract attention. Let me also assure you, Lord Littlecote, that there's no need to put yourself in a taking over a quite innocent desire for privacy. Though we hadn't yet got round to the subject before your arrival, I would wager everything I own that Miss Hawtry here merely wished to discuss my art collection."

"Art collection be damned. Never even knew you had one."

"Well, you seem to be the only person in London who doesn't know of it. I can assure you, it's the talk of the town."

"And does the town also go behind chimney pots to discuss it?"

"Oh, we're back to that, then, are we? Well, come along, Miss Hawtry. He's right, you know. No need to skulk while we exchange aesthetic opinions. Besides, it must be time for the fireworks. Ah, yes, what did I tell you? There's the first salvo now.''

It was a pity, Mary Anne thought as she went to stand next to Sydney and gaze absently at the breathtaking spectacle in the sky, that the extravaganzas of a lifetime had to be taking place at a point when she was completely absorbed with her own problems.

The fireworks in Hyde Park had been preempted by her run-in with Mr. Wakley. Now a mounting sense of foreboding was causing her to watch this pyrotechnic display with less appreciation than she usually accorded the routine appearance of the Big Dipper. Years from now when her grandchildren asked about the fabled peace celebration, she'd have nothing at all she could tell them. But then, Mary Anne dismally reminded herself, that was one embarrassment she would successfully avoid since she seemed fated not to marry.

A fiery comet spiraling in high flight all of a sudden exploded into a myriad red, white, and blue blazing stars that shot off in all directions, danced ensemble for a moment, and then came raining down. The 'aahs' and 'oohs' that followed that display gave Mary Anne the chance to breathe in Sydney's ear, ''I need to talk to you.'' Only Anthony took his eyes off the heavens to give the sisters a curious glance as Mary Anne once more led the way toward the chimney pot.

''What's come over you?'' Sydney inquired crossly. ''You seem fascinated with this spot.''

''Let's not go tonight.'' Mary Anne's words came tumbling out. ''To Lord Linley's, I mean. I was trying to discover what he's up to, but then Roderick came blundering in before I could question him. But I'm afraid, Sydney. For I just know he's up to some sort of devilry.''

''Linley? Naturally. That's a foregone conclusion.''

"Please don't make jokes. I know that neither of our thieves—not that Anthony's really a— Oh, never mind all that. What I mean to say is, just because no one discovered that odious painting during either break-in doesn't mean that Linley won't produce the thing tonight."

"Oh, I'm quite convinced he will."

"You are? Well then, that settles it. We mustn't go. Make some excuse. You're good at that sort of thing. Say, for instance, that Savannah's ill."

"What a wonderful suggestion," Sydney replied dryly, "since Maxwell paraded her before our guests earlier this evening."

"Well, then you think of something. Say you've got the headache."

"I can assure you I never felt better in my entire life."

"Sydney, you can't go! You can't let Lord Linley flaunt that shocking portrait in front of Maxwell."

"Why ever not?" Sydney stared toward the balustrade where Mrs. Edleston was tiptoeing to make some remark in Sir Maxwell's ear. "I'm actually looking forward to this evening. In fact, I shall quite die of disappointment if the portrait isn't there. Now excuse me, little sister. I musn't miss a moment of this historic evening."

Mary Anne suppressed a groan and followed her sister back into the group to stare up sightlessly at the sky. She was too preoccupied to note that from force of habit she'd gone to stand next to Anthony for a refuge.

But when the fireworks were finally over and the party had gone on to St. James's Street, she was ready to believe she'd allowed a morbid imagination to run rampant. From the moment they crossed his threshold, Lord Linley seemed at special pains to play the gracious host. And Lord Linley in this role was, for Mary Anne at least, a revelation.

For the first time she was able to understand why he was

so sought after in the withdrawing rooms of the social set and just what it was that had attracted Sydney to him in the first place. His wit sparkled like the star showers created by roman candles. He was indeed a polished raconteur. And this time, a first in Mary Anne's experience, his anecdotes were free of all the malice that had seemed their chief ingredient.

His conversation had to do with family foibles, memories he and his cousin shared. He had his guests in stitches as he recalled how "little Maxwell" had "borrowed" an irate great-uncle's ear trumpet and used it for a bugle to sound the charge. For the first time that evening, Sir Maxwell seemed to relax and laugh along with everybody else.

"We could have used it at Vitoria, sir." Anthony chuckles, and the general agreed.

"Now that reminds me—" Lord Linley was well launched into another boyhood anecdote when supper was announced. "Oh, well. I'll finish my tale at the table. Let's see how. Mrs. Edleston has graciously agreed to act as hostess. As guest of honor, Max, you shall take her in." He offered his arm to Sydney then, while he directed, "Lord Littlecote, you take in Lady Barbara, trailed by our Prussian guests. Pray forgive me for not having the proper match of male and female, but we did wish to be *en famille*, you'll recall. Now then, Captain, you escort Miss Hawtry, and we shall soon discover whether my chef will put me to the blush for all my extravagant claims about his genius."

It was a merry party that made its way toward the dining room. But when Mary Anne realized they must file through the picture gallery on their way there, all her apprehensions rushed back full force. The first quick glance almost convinced her that Sydney's portrait wasn't there. Even so, her head swiveled back and forth as they passed through the long, narrow corridor.

"For God's sake, relax, won't you," Anthony said in her ear. "I told you it's not here. You look like Lady Macbeth seeing imaginary daggers."

"That wasn't Lady—" she'd begun when Lord Linley turned back toward them. "Mustn't dillydally," he said. "We'll view my modest collection later on. I'll admit to an eagerness to show it off. It's created a small stir among art patrons. I know that Miss Hawtry, especially, has worked up quite an interest."

When they entered the dining room, a footman with a taper in his hand quickly stepped away from the mahogany table. All eyes riveted upon its centerpiece. A ring of sparklers encircled a gold-plated replica of the Temple of Concord that the Regent had erected in Green Park. The guests gasped with delight, then broke into spontaneous applause.

"Oh, do you like it?" The host beamed with pleasure. "Actually, I had it made for you, Max. Souvenir of the peace celebration, don't you know. Didn't seem quite right for Wellington to collect all the spoils of victory. Our family, too, has done its part for England." As Anthony held a chair for her, Mary Anne could hardly believe she was in such charity with Lord Linley.

It was obvious from the start that his lordship's chef scorned the conventional idea of a simple supper consisting of cold meats, sweets, fruit, and wine. The menu outdid even the most lavish dinners Mary Anne had been exposed to. True, there was not a soup course, but the table groaned under an artistically dressed array.

There were soles and flounders, shrimp, partridges, pheasants, hares. A collar of brawn was garnished with French lilies. Young pig, mushroom in a sauce béchamel, oysters, lobsters, cod, a haunch of venison, apples, and chocolates completed the bill of fare.

No sooner were the guests seated than the footmen stepped

forward to fill their wineglasses with claret. And as they helped themselves to the lavish array, their host resumed the anecdote that had been interrupted in the drawing room.

Mary Anne was listening and smiling, savoring a shrimp, when she felt Anthony suddenly go rigid. She glanced curiously his way. But his face was expressionless, and his eyes were fixed upon his heaped-up plate.

A reawakened sense of foreboding forced her to look toward the opposite wall for a clue to his odd behavior. The unfortunate thing was that as she did so she was reaching for her glass of claret. The shock caused her to upset it and send its contents spilling across the table.

"Congratulations," Anthony said beneath his breath as he leapt up to save his white satin knee smalls from the red tide running toward them. A footman sprang to the rescue with a cloth; Mary Anne smiled a weak smile of apology and the meal continued. The only evidence that any of the other diners recognized the source of her distress was a small smile of satisfaction upon Lord Linley's face.

The younger Prussian was practicing his English with a mostly unintelligible account of a dinner for King Frederick he'd attended. The thrust of the narrative seemed to be that the bill of fare suffered in comparison to their present feast.

While all eyes were upon Count Roethke, Mary Anne risked a surreptitious peek. How could she or anyone have missed the portrait? It expanded before her horrified eyes to the size of a cricket field. The reclining figure on the canvas might just as well have been shouting rather than silently contemplating a bunch of grapes.

Still, though, she reassured herself as Anthony's sharp kick upon her ankle warned her to look elsewhere, paintings were a commonplace and Sydney's was not the only one in the Grecian style that this room boasted. Hadn't that been a temple ruin on its other side? Perhaps no one else would notice that the goddess—or whatever—in that shocking state of nature had her sister's face.

And perhaps pigs might fly.

Mary Anne tried an oyster as the most likely tidbit to travel safely down her constricted throat. She choked immediately.

"Are you all right, m'dear?" Lord Linley's voice was solicitous; his eyes gleamed with malicious glee. "Bring some water," Sir Maxwell said in a low voice to a footman, and after she'd swallowed a bit Mary Anne managed to smile wanly at the company. They were all gazing at her rather oddly.

"Why don't you just stand up and point?" Anthony whispered, and the meal continued.

She might as well do so, she thought, for now she understood the evening's entertainment. Their host was playing his own private game of cat and mouse. He had skillfully seen to it that no one should notice the painting prematurely. Like an accomplished conjurer he had focused attention upon the table, concealing the trick still up his sleeve. It was amusing to allow the guests to discover his artwork one by one while he quietly observed their reactions. Well, she and Anthony had already been picked off like two pheasants at a shoot. And she was sure of one thing—if the other victims at the table did not rise from cover, Lord Linley would certainly find a way to flush them out.

Sydney was the next to spy the painting. Mary Anne could not see her face, but she heard a low laugh that sounded genuinely amused, followed by an aside to her host. "Well, Linley, I see the suspense is over."

Mrs. Edleston, seated at the foot of the table, must have noted the direction of Sydney's eyes. Mary Anne watched in mesmerized fascination as the older woman's head turned toward the wall. "Oh, what a lovely painting, Lord Linley," she called out ingenuously. "Who is the artist? I don't re-call—" She froze suddenly, aghast.

All heads now faced the painting, Lady Barbara, Lord Littlecote and the Prussians having turned around to see it.

It's like a tableau, Mary Anne thought. We've all changed to statues.

Still, somewhere in her detached consciousness some critic was at work admiring the translucence of the flesh tones, the seductiveness of her sister's lovely face. If she were a stranger to the subject and had merely chanced upon the work in some gallery, she would have paused before it, drinking in its beauty. But the subject was her sister. And this was no gallery. It was the residence of a reputed rake.

Sir Maxwell was the first member of the tableau to un-freeze. Mary Anne held her breath as he replaced the glass he'd been holding to his lips down upon the table with a steady hand. He slowly turned his head toward his host and cousin and their gazes locked. "Well, Linley," he said in a tone that could almost pass for casual, "I can see the quality of your art collection has not been exaggerated. It's even—"

But whatever Sir Maxwell had planned to say was sud-denly drowned out by a mighty roar—an eruption of mixed rage and indignation. "You miserable, foppish cad, how dare you!" Lord Littlecote sprang from his chair and overturned it.

He fell upon Lord Linley in a rush that no one could pos-sibly have anticipated. He grabbed the dandy by the throat, his hands a bulldog's jaws. He shook his victim like a terrier. Two footmen leapt to their master's aid, but Anthony was quicker. He began prizing Littlecote's hands loose while at the same time he tried to restore his berserk lordship to his senses.

"I know how you feel, Littlecote. Wouldn't mind throt-tling this scum myself, but, really, he's hardly worth swinging for.'' His muscles strained as he broke loose the death grip. Lord Linley collapsed back in his chair, gasping for breath under the ministrations of his servants.

Littlecote redirected his wrath upon Captain Rodes. ''How dare you interfere! How dare you stop me from wringing that villain's neck! And it's no good your saying you know how I feel. It ain't *your* fiancée's picture taking up half a wall— with barely a stitch on.'' He lunged for his host again while Anthony struggled to retain him. ''It's my fiancée he's flaunting naked like some Covent Garden whore.''

Mary Anne gasped, then turned fiery red as all eyes focused on her. The guests had all sprung to their feet when Littlecote attacked. Now they began to dart surreptitious glances back and forth between her and the portrait.

She stole another peek herself, not wishing to turn and stare. Well, yes, she supposed it could be mistaken fairly easily for her. Especially by an already suspicious gentleman who would not wear his spectacles in public.

''Oh, really, Lord Littlecote.'' The former amusement in Sydney's voice had heightened. ''As much as I applaud your quixotic attack on our host here, I must assure you you are operating under a grave misapprehension. Mary Anne is not the subject of the painting. If you'll look a bit more closely, you'll realize that I am.''

''That's quite unnecessary, Sydney.'' Mary Anne's voice rang out bravely as she threw her character to the winds in the hope of saving her sister's marriage. ''I do appreciate what you are trying to do for me, but of course Lord Littlecote is right. It is my portrait. Though I must say that when I sat—er, that is, *lay*—I mean to say *reclined* for it, I never thought it would wind up—that is to say—''

''That will do, Mary Anne.'' General Sir Maxwell Cunliffe did not raise his voice. But nonetheless it carried with it the heavy weight of command. He strode purposefully around the table and removed the painting from the wall. "No matter who's the subject, it's clear this belongs in my household. Linley, you may keep the Temple of Concord,"—he gave an ironic twist to the harmonious title—"in payment for this. You alone know the relative worth of the two items. If necessary, you may bill me."

Lord Linley, still slumped in his chair, removed one hand from massaging his throat and waved it dismissively. There was a triumphant smile on the handsome, jaded face. "Oh, consider the portrait a gift, Max," he managed to rasp. "Wouldn't dream of charging you for it, old boy. After all, I've had full value."

"I'm sure you have, Cousin," Maxwell replied softly. He then went striding from the room, carrying the huge artwork, while the others, hardly knowing which way to look, trailed along behind him.

Their two carriages were waiting. Mary Anne saw to it that she rode in the same one as Sir Maxwell, who had handed the portrait over to his impassive coachman. The other passengers were Mrs. Edleston and Marshal Von Ziefen. The Prussian looked bemused, as if he had understood nothing of all the high drama that had just transpired. Mrs. Edleston appeared distressed. *I suppose she loves him, too.* The irrelevant thought somehow managed to insinuate itself among all the turmoil seething in Mary Anne's mind.

Except for the clatter of wheels and horses' hooves upon the cobblestones, they rode in silence for a bit. Mary Anne tried to screw up her courage. It was now or never if she was going to set Sir Maxwell's mind at rest.

She began in a voice that was pitched far too high and woefully inclined to quaver. "I can't tell you how very sorry I am, sir, to be the cause of so much embarrassment. I should never have posed for such an—ah—indelicate painting. I realize it now. But please believe me, I had never intended it to be seen by anyone."

The fact that the general laughed dryly here was a bit off-putting, but she persevered.

"No, truly. You must believe me. The last thing I wanted was for it to fall into the clutches of that—that—of your cousin. But Lord Linley tricked me into wagering it at cards. You must understand I never meant—"

"I do understand." Sir Maxwell's voice was heavy. Fatigue seemed to have taken over any other emotions he might have felt. "I understand only too well, Mary Anne, what it is you're trying to do. And while I greatly admire your loyalty to your sister, I have to tell you it won't hold water. While your resemblance to Sydney is quite strong, m'dear, you must admit it strains credulity to believe both you and she have beauty marks in the precise spot upon your breast. No, Mary Anne, my wife, not you, is the subject of that cursed painting."

# Chapter
# Eighteen

*The peace celebration was over. The parades and* fireworks, the tableaux and mock sea battles, might never have happened, Mary Anne thought as she walked with Savannah in Hyde Park on a duck-feeding expedition. London had returned, almost with relief, to normalcy. The only reminder of the recent festivity was the devastation to the grass and foilage the trampling populace had left behind. A benevolent Mother Nature was slowly at work, however, erasing even that.

It was a pity she could not do as much for all their trampled lives. Mary smiled wryly to herself as her niece let go her hand to go chasing after a squirrel. The climax of a celebration staged to usher in a new era of harmony had for the Hawtry sisters signaled instead the end of all their hopes and dreams.

The very night of his cousin's disastrous supper party General Sir Maxwell Cunliffe had moved out of his house. The following day he'd sent for his things, and the direction given to the servants was Mrs. Edleston's hired residence.

And since they had been, after all, the general's guests, Lady Barbara Kennet and Captain Anthony Rodes shortly thereafter took their leave, with profuse and embarrassed thank yous to their hostess.

How much or how little of what had happened the two Prussian gentlemen understood remained a mystery. But they also left on the heels of the others, ostensibly because the celebration was now over and it was time for them to be returning home. In actuality, they stayed on in London. Mary Anne had spied them once in a large party of horsemen trotting along on Rotten Row.

Lord Littlecote had been the exception to this general tactfulness. The morning following the debacle he had insisted upon an early interview with Mary Anne. His lordship was red-faced with indignation and quite obviously felt the need to vent his spleen. His mama had been right. He had been poised on the verge of a disastrous misalliance. But, thank God, his eyes had been opened in the nick of time. And as far as he was concerned it made damned little difference just which sister had posed in the nude. He wanted no alliance with such a rackety family in any case. It was as plain as the nose on his face that when Sir Maxwell Cunliffe severed his connection, it was a signal to the polite world that the Hawtry females were now well beyond the pale.

"But on the other hand, Sir Maxwell, who has moved in with his mistress, is a pattern card of virtue, I collect."

"Can you blame him!" Littlecote had thundered.

"No," she'd answered wearily. "Right now I don't think I can blame anyone for anything."

Lord Littlecote had gone on to inform her that he would

put a notice in the *Gazette* immediately to the effect that their betrothal was at an end. "Of course I'll put it about that you cried off," he'd added magnanimously. "It's the chivalrous thing to do. Doubt anyone will believe it, though. Your sister's character is bound to be in shreds."

If that was so, Mary Anne now thought cynically, it hadn't made Sydney any less sought after than before. More so, in fact. For the hostesses still left in London fell over one another to send her cards, eager to observe how the beauty would conduct herself now that she'd been openly abandoned by her husband.

And Sydney had responded by accepting as many of the invitations as seemed reasonable, holding her head up high while ignoring as best she could the innuendos about her husband's new domestic arrangements.

It was much easier to deal with questions concerning Lord Linley's whereabouts. Here Sydney did not have to feign an ignorance. It was truly news to her that the dandy had left London to join the ranks of the British who were converging upon Paris, now that that city was once more open to them.

"All the world's in Paris," a popular song proclaimed. Fashionable ladies longed to know what was being worn there. Rakes and dandies went to look at the Parisienne belles. Starved English palates yearned for French food and wine. Art lovers were eager to examine the treasure Napoléon had looted from the vanquished nations to grace the museums of his capital. Lord Linley was no doubt in his element these days, Mary Anne reflected. And none the worse for wear.

It was only the lives of the Hawtry sisters that were now a shambles. She sighed to herself as Savannah gave up on the squirrel and fixed her mind once again on the more receptive ducks. As they continued their walk toward the water, she tried to believe that in time they, too, would come to terms with all that had happened and piece together their broken lives, never mind that some cracks would always show.

In actuality, the process was already beginning. Sydney had insisted that Mary Anne make her home at Cunliffe House. "Maxwell is far too much the gentleman to divorce me, even if he had the grounds he thinks he has. Nor will he likely cut off my allowance. So I can easily support us both. And God knows I need you. But far more importantly, so does Savannah."

So, she had stayed. Not that there had been much choice. Their mother would hardly have been overjoyed to have a younger woman living with her, evoking comparisons. But the truth was, Mary Anne seemed incapable of planning for herself just yet. Perhaps once Anthony's and Lady Barbara's marriage was an accomplished fact . . . She resolutely pushed that bleak thought from her mind. In the meantime, as Sydney had pointed out, there was Savannah.

The little girl had been bewildered by the general's sudden disappearance. The litany she'd learned when a portrait was the only father she knew was now recalled to explain his absence and the pervading unhappiness throughout the house. "Papa—soldier," she repeated over and over until they all could scream.

Mary Anne had done her best to divert the child. There were frequent doll tea parties. She'd brought home a kitten from the stable. They'd gone to the Tower of London to see the menagerie. But the best treat of all was still the expedition through Hyde Park to feed the eagerly awaiting ducks.

Mary Anne watched tenderly as the little girl, with absorbed intensity, scattered her bread crumbs, trying, ineffectually, to see to it that the smaller, weaker fowl also got their share.

"All gone," she announced sadly to the flock when her bag was empty. These fair-weather friends promptly turned their feathery tails and took once more to the water.

Thus deserted, they amused themselves as best they could with any other diversions they could find till Mary Anne was forced to say, "We'd best be getting back. Cook will have your supper ready."

She had planned to leave the park before the fashionable hour. London was rapidly thinning of company, but the remaining members of the *ton* still rode out at five to see and be seen. The prospect of Lady Barbara and Anthony being among their number was enough to make Mary Anne pick up the child and walk rapidly along the footpath that flanked the carriage drive.

She glanced warily over her shoulder at the sound of an approaching carriage and then relaxed. It was not the high-perch phaeton in which she'd once seen Captain Rodes tooling about the town. Instead, a coachman-driven barouche clattered into view. Her relief was short-lived, though, for as the carriage drew abreast she spied Sir Maxwell and Mrs. Edleston among the laughing group.

Their attention was fixed upon a portly gentleman who was spinning some sort of tale, so they did not glance toward the young woman and the child. Mary Anne was not as fortunate, however, in her attempt to divert Savannah. The little girl saw her papa in the carriage and began to cry after him as the barouche went speeding out of sight.

Suddenly Mary Anne saw red. It was one thing for a group of sap-skulled adults to make themselves miserable. But when the little ones were made to suffer for their stupidity—well, by Jupiter, it was the outside of enough! And she for one would not stand for it.

The next morning as she walked down Wimpole Street Mary Anne tried very hard to maintain the same level of indignation. But the fact of the matter was that her heart was in her mouth. To help screw up her courage she had dressed with unusual care. Her walking costume consisted of a pale peach muslin round dress topped with a white-striped lute-string spencer. She wore white kid shoes, straw-colored gloves, and a broad-brimmed leghorn hat trimmed in peach satin. But the ensemble failed to boost her confidence. It was all she could do to mount the front steps of Mrs. Edleston's residence and ply the knocker.

"Sir Maxwell has not yet risen." The toplofty butler's expression underscored the solecism of arriving long before the prescribed hour for morning calls.

"Then wake him," she managed to retort. "Tell him Miss Hawtry wishes to see him on a matter of grave importance. He'll see me, I've no doubt." She pushed past the major-domo into the marble entry hall.

She had barely seated herself in the cramped parlor where the butler had left her and had just begun to wonder how much of its garish decor was a reflection of Mrs. Edleston's taste or whether it could be laid at the door of the house's absent owner, when Sir Maxwell hurried into the room. His hair was still tousled from the pillow (in a bed shared with Mrs. Edleston? she wondered). He was in the act of tying the belt to his gold brocade dressing gown and was still unshaven. "What's wrong, Mary Anne? Has something happened to Savannah?"

Whether it was the deep anxiety etched upon his face or his state of dishabille that accounted for her transformation was not a matter Mary Anne stopped to analyze. She only knew she'd suddenly lost her awe of General Sir Maxwell Cunliffe.

"Of course something's happened to Savannah," she snapped, then hastened on as he went pale under the salt-and-pepper stubble of his beard. "Oh, I don't mean she's ill or anything like that. But she's lost her father—and her mother's miserable—and she's just a baby and doesn't understand—not that being an adult makes it any easier to understand why two seemingly intelligent people have to act like such ninnyhammers."

"I'm sorry if Savannah is being hurt by all this," he answered stiffly. "But she's only known me for a small portion of her short life. She's just a baby. She'll soon get over it."

"She will not! I was not much older than she when my father died, and I'm still not over it."

"I'm sorry. But under the circumstances, there's little I can do, is there?"

"There's a lot you can do! And will you please sit down? For I plan to ring a peal over you, and it's hard enough to get up the courage to do so without having to strain my neck in the process."

"And just why should I submit to being lectured by a flighty beauty barely out of the schoolroom?"

The question was reasonable, but nonetheless Sir Maxwell did sit down.

"Because there's no one else to do so. Savannah's too little to talk sense to you. My sister has too much pride to defend herself. And who else is going to lecture a general?"

"I wouldn't know about Sydney's pride. But I do know this—she's far too intelligent to defend the indefensible. I was willing to wear blinders where most of her behavior was concerned. After all . . ."—he shrugged ruefully—"when one marries a beauty years younger than oneself, then goes abroad and leaves her to her own devices, one can hardly expect her to lead a cloistered life. But what one can expect is a certain amount of discretion, which was not forthcoming. Believe me, there were plenty of people eager to fill me in on the wild life she was leading.''

''And did you happen to notice that the so-called wildness never took place until Mrs. Edleston had followed you to the Peninsula?''

''That was hardly my doing,'' he answered stiffly, and Mary Anne sniffed in lieu of rebuttal.

''But be that as it may, nothing can excuse having such a painting displayed upon another man's wall. The most tolerant husband in all the world could hardly be expected to turn a blind eye to a thing like that.''

''He might if he'd bothered to find out that the portrait was actually painted for him.''

''Oh, indeed? And Linley hung it in his dining room, displayed to all comers, as a personal favor to me, I collect.''

''It hadn't been displayed to all comers,'' she protested. ''I know that for a fact. Two different persons broke in to—uh—retrieve it, and it wasn't hung at all.''

''Really, Mary Anne . . .''—he began to rise—''what my cousin chooses to do with his art collection is of no interest to me. I have yet to have my breakfast.''

''Don't you dare get up till you've heard me out,'' she stormed, and much to her surprise he sank back down into his chair once more. ''Now listen carefully. Whether you believe me or not, Sydney did have that odious painting done for you. She'd heard about Mrs. Edleston following you to Portugal, you see. She knew you'd only married her for her beauty, and she feared you'd forgot what she used to look like. For you'd only seen her breeding those last few months when you were home.''

''Didn't she know she'd never been lovelier to me than

she was then?" he interposed wearily. "I certainly told her so."

"Well, even if it happened to be true, of course she didn't believe it. People only believe their preconceived notions. At least that's been my experience. And hers was that you would only remember her as a baby hippo, and she wished you to see the real Sydney." Mary Anne blushed. "A great deal of the real Sydney. The trouble began when she confided in Lord Linley that she'd done so."

Mary Anne went on to explain how her sister had been cozened into wagering the portrait at cards. "By the by," she concluded, "just what did you do to make your cousin hate you so?"

"A lot, I collect, now I look back on it." Sir Maxwell seemed to be thinking aloud. "I was older. Always held up by the family as an example for him. Then, too, I remember taking his part more than once at school. When the other boys picked on him for his missish ways, I sailed in and thrashed them."

"Well, that was certainly no reason to hate you," she said indignantly.

"Wasn't it? I rather think in his mind it was. At any rate, the last straw would have been when our uncle left me the fortune our aunt had led him to believe he'd inherit. Yes, Linley had plenty of cause to wish to score over me."

"Well, if you're right, and you must be, no wonder he was so eager to get his hands on that painting. And I frankly don't blame you," she said candidly, "if you choose not to believe Sydney could be taken in so. I found it rather hard to swallow myself. Sydney's always been such a knowing 'un. But if I've learned anything of late, it's that being in love does terrible things to the judgment. Then, too," she mused, "think of that horrible supper he gave. Even knowing him for what he was, until I realized it was all staged in order to get full shock value from the painting, I'll admit I was taken in and actually found Lord Linley quite charming. Anyhow, I've told you exactly what happened. You can choose to believe it all or not."

"You are saying, then, Mary Anne, that even though Sydney was in love with my cousin, she actually had the painting done for me?" He shook his head to try and clear it.

"No!" Really, he was too exasperating. "Pray pay attention. Of course she didn't love that—that—well, never mind. He *is* your cousin. But, you pea-goose, it's you Sydney's in love with. And has been, she said, from the moment she first saw you cross the dance floor at Almack's to engage her for the cotillion. Then everybody made the mistake of thinking she'd married you for your fortune. Including me," she added ingenuously.

"And me," he echoed softly.

"Well, she didn't. But of course no one will believe that a Hawtry could be anything other than a fortune hunter. But she would actually have thrown her cap over the windmill for you, she said. Later, of course, she learned that Mrs. Edleston had already done so."

He reddened. "That business never had any bearing on my marriage. Mrs. Edleston and I go a long, long way back."

"Not back far enough. When Sydney saw you kissing her in the Carlton House gardens, that's when the fat was really in the fire. I still think we could have kept you from seeing the portrait somehow. But at that point she wanted you to see it and think exactly what you thought. And I don't know as I blame her. You'd no right to flaunt your mistress in front of her that way."

"I wasn't doing anything of the kind. I know this is hardly

chivalrous. Especially under the circumstances.'' He gazed uncomfortably around Mrs. Edelston's parlor. "But that kiss you saw, well, I was on the receiving end. I'd just told the lady I'd not be seeing her again.''

"I see.'' Mary Anne also gave their surroundings a speaking look.

"No, you don't,'' he retorted. "Not that I can blame you for your assumption.''

"What I think has nothing to say in the matter.'' Mary Anne stood up. "I only wished to make sure you know the truth about that horrid painting—which should have been told you in the first place. What you do now is up to you, of course. But I'll tell you this much, you've no right to make little Savannah cry after you. And if you have any sense of duty at all—that's not tied up with king and country, I mean to say—you'll go back with your family where you belong. And that's what I came to tell you.'' She moved toward the door. "And I do hope you will forgive my plain speaking, Sir Maxwell,'' she added formally.

"I just possibly may manage that.'' When he smiled, he looked positively boyish. And in spite of his tousled hair and stubbled chin—or perhaps because of it—Mary Anne could now see why her sister had found him irresistible. The matter was even easier to comprehend when he crushed her in a rib-cracking bear hug and planted an enthusiastic kiss upon her forehead. "You're a pearl without price, little sister, did you know it?'' he said huskily.

Mary Anne was so astonished by this reaction that when, on her way to the stairs, she passed Mrs. Edleston clad in a pale pink dressing gown looking less than pleased to see her there, she merely gave the widow a civil nod instead of the stinging set-down she'd rehearsed for ages.

\* \* \*

As she walked through the park toward home, her thoughts were in such a turmoil that she'd actually been staring hard at the black-and-white bird for ages without registering its significance. Then the sound of approaching hoofbeats caused it to fly off the low-hanging branch of the oak tree it was perched upon.

"Oh, no! Not again!" Mary Anne groaned. She began to look frantically around her.

"What are you doing out here so early—and all alone?" Captain Rodes inquired as he reined his stallion to a halt beside her.

"Looking for a second magpie."

"Well, that makes sense," he observed to the heavens as he dismounted.

"It does actually. It's bad luck to see only one, you know. All my recent troubles seemed to start with a single magpie. And now just when things appear to be taking a turn for the better—"

Before she stopped to consider the propriety of the thing, she was pouring out the story of her recent interview with Sir Maxwell. "So you see," she concluded, "I do believe he intends to return home to his family, and I don't want anything to jinx their chance for happiness this time. So it's imperative to find that second magpie."

"Yes, I do see what you mean," he said solemnly. "I'll help you look."

"That's most kind of you," she replied as she turned in all directions, her head tilted toward trees and sky. During one of her revolutions her glance swept across him and then reverted. "You aren't looking," she accused.

It was true. His eyes were fastened on her, and there was a light in them she'd not seen since his disastrous proposal. She gazed back in some confusion. "There's something different about you," she blurted. She looked closely at the clothing he was wearing. It was marvelous what superb tailoring did for a man, and Anthony, with his broad shoulders and trim waist, was certainly Weston's ideal customer. But no, she'd seen that dark blue riding coat before, so that couldn't be it. Then suddenly it struck her. "You've shaved off your mustache!"

"Oh, yes, that." He felt his upper lip. "I only grew the thing because Lady Barbara had a preference for 'em. But now that our engagement's off, there seemed no need to keep it."

She was not at all convinced she'd heard him right. "Your engagement's off? Oh, Anthony, are you sure?"

"Positive. Lady Barbara cried off last night. I was on my way to Cunliffe House to break the news."

"But why on earth would she do a sap-skulled thing like that?"

"Thank you," he grinned. "She had a pair of reasons, actually. The first was that Littlecote had confided you'd said you were in love with someone else. He thought you meant Lord Linley. She wasn't quite so dense, though. She concluded it was me. And she'd further decided I was in love with you as well."

"She actually thought *that*?"

"Oh, yes. But that wasn't the chief reason she cried off. It only made things easier for her. The point is, she wishes to marry someone else."

"Roderick!" Mary Anne crowed and clapped her hands. "She wishes to marry Roderick! Just wait till I tell Sydney. By George, I pulled it off!"

"No, actually you didn't. Oh, I realize you were throwing her at his head, or vice versa. But as much as I hate to disappoint you, it's not your Littlecote she wishes to marry."

"It's not? Well then, who is it?"

"Count Roethke."

"The Prussian?"

"Yes." He grinned. "And all the time we thought she was merely translating our conversations for him. It appears they were saying a whole lot more."

"Oh, Anthony!" She beamed up at him and then looked conscience-stricken. "I do hope you don't mind too much."

"Well now, I was rather counting on you to help mend my broken heart," he said huskily as he took her in his arms.

The kiss was long overdue and ardent. And when their lips finally parted and she leaned against him breathlessly, "Oh, Anthony," she confided to his shoulder, "there must be another magpie around here somewhere."

"Bound to be. Whole flocks of 'em, all flying two by two," he murmured as he raised her chin and began kissing her again.

When they reluctantly drew apart the second time, she looked up at him earnestly and asked, "Now will you finally believe that when I told Roderick I no longer wished to be betrothed to him, I really didn't know about your fortune?"

He ran a finger tenderly down the side of her face. "Let's bury the past, love. Along with my stiff-necked pride. None of that makes the slightest bit of difference now."

No, she sighed to herself as they walked slowly toward home with Anthony leading his horse by the bridle, he still doesn't believe I can love him for himself. Then as they approached Hyde Park Corner she spied Sir Maxwell leaping down from his curricle in front of Cunliffe House. The general tossed his reins to his tiger and ran eagerly up the steps.

Well, actually, Mary Anne reflected, Anthony was

quite right to say it made no difference. For he, like Sir Maxwell, would discover the truth in time. Gentlemen were, after all, notorious slow-tops when it came to matters of the heart.

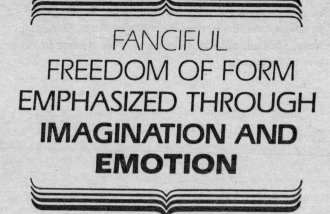

# FANCIFUL
# FREEDOM OF FORM
# EMPHASIZED THROUGH
# IMAGINATION AND
# EMOTION

# Marian Devon

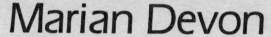